Élise Turcotte

translated by
Rhonda Mullins

Guyana

Coach House Books, Toronto

Canada Council   Conseil des Arts    ONTARIO ARTS COUNCIL   Canada
for the Arts   du Canada   CONSEIL DES ARTS DE L'ONTARIO

Published with the generous assistance of the Canada Council for the Arts, especially through the Translation Program, and the Ontario Arts Council. Coach House Books also acknowledges the support of the Government of Canada through the Canada Book Fund and the Government of Ontario.

LIBRARY AND ARCHIVES CANADA CATALOGUING IN PUBLICATION

Turcotte, Elise
[Guyana. English]
    Guyana / Élise Turcotte ; translated by Rhonda Mullins.

Translation of French book with same title.
Issued in print and electronic formats.
ISBN 978-1-55245-292-9 (pbk.).

I. Mullins, Rhonda, 1966-, translator II. Title. III. Guyana. English.

PS8589.U62G8913 2014   C843'.54   C2013-907673-5

Guyana is available as an ebook: ISBN 978 1 77056 373 5

Purchase of the print version of this book entitles you to a free digital copy. To claim your ebook of this title, please email sales@chbooks.com with proof of purchase or visit chbooks.com/digital. (Coach House Books reserves the right to terminate the free digital download offer at any time.)

She became a ghost. What is a ghost? A being that puts you under its spell? That you can't escape? How did she disappear? Is there even an answer to that question?

— Åke Edwardson

The Wings of Invention

There was still something I needed to sort out.

School was ending soon, my year of battle would end with it, and I wanted everything to be perfect. But there was something nagging at me, making me feel like I hadn't finished my homework. The slightest stumbling block can foretell dark days to come. But I was born to survive, as others are born to thrive in absence or in the hereafter.

I dialled the number, swearing it would be my last try.

I had been calling for three days, with no answer, not even Harriet's recorded voice. I was starting to get annoyed. It was a business, after all, and I was a good customer.

Why weren't they answering?

One last try. Then I would hang up for good.

Except I couldn't.

I listened to the ringing with the attention of a soldier awaiting orders.

And then the dread of something more final started to insinuate itself in me. The ringing started to reverberate inside me as if I were in an empty room, on the eve of a departure.

Maybe the hair salon was closed, but that didn't seem likely. I realized that if anything had happened to her, I would never know. If she had gone to work somewhere else, I wouldn't be able to find her. I didn't even know her last name. I had never asked.

Philippe wanted an appointment with Kimi and that was that. His hair was sticking out in tufts at the back of his neck, and he didn't like it. His obsession was going to take him over, and soon he would feel like a metamorphosis had begun. His own body was a source of so many questions: his body, the world – leaving him feeling like he was being sucked up by an unknown force.

That morning he had asked me to call one more time.

'My hair, Mom,' he pleaded.

I was dreading the moment when I would have to tell him that we might have to find someone else.

Philippe's hair is a serious matter. More serious still is accepting the touch of a stranger. Kimi understood that at our first appointment. Her gestures naturally moulded to Philippe's standoffish ways. We were both grieving, and Kimi had a gift: with just one look, she wrapped us in gentle certainty. She immediately became one of the new markers we were counting on to help us get on with our lives.

The scene had unfolded the same way for over a year:

She would sit him in the chair, gently drape his shoulders in the black cape that he would pull down over his thighs to smooth out the folds while she fastened the snap at the neck. I would stand behind them, and she would shoot me a glance in the mirror, smiling, and make a comment about Philippe's big eyes. The haircut had to bring out his eyes. Once she started cutting, I would sit down beside them. I would swivel in the chair and flip through magazines. Hair would fall onto the beige linoleum. Philippe would relax. I would talk to Kimi. Was Philippe listening? I didn't know. He would study his face in the mirror, watch the hairdresser's gestures, sometimes show a hint of a smile. He would sit up tall and stay quiet. More like concentrated, really, as if on a math problem. At the end, when Kimi would take the electric shaver from the drawer, we would both be silent. How I would have loved to run the shaver over his whole head. Philippe would brace himself a bit at the buzzing. Things slip, don't they? Hands can grow weak, and composure can vanish under a drop of blood behind the ear. But then, no, the haircut was done. Kimi would warm the gel a little in the palm of her hand. Despite Philippe's wary eye, she would ruffle his hair. This was too much for him, but he was too proud not to let her. Then he would remove the cape, suddenly in a hurry to be off. Aside from Kimi, nothing could keep us in the salon. I would go on talking to her while she swept up the fallen hair. This was my favourite part: the broom gliding gently over the floor, the hair gathered into a pile, a compact blotch you want to touch. But you don't. Touching it would be like sullying your hands with something freshly dead. I prefer things that are properly done, clean, in a neat pile. This was why I didn't like hanging around too long in the salon, which was anything but neat and tidy. When the ball of hair was neatly tucked against the wall, I would pay and follow Philippe out.

This scene was an enclave of peace in a series of more complicated efforts for Philippe and me: the decision, the phone call, the bike ride, how to position the bike locks, who should open the door... People have no idea the discussions that can go on in accomplishing a series of mundane tasks with a child. We also had to walk through the wall of young locals hanging around on the sidewalk in front of the salon, or sitting lined up in chairs, as if in a movie set in a village in the West Indies. I say this because of Kimi. I can almost see the colour of the weather change, from grey-white or cold blue to a warmer hue. I'm arranging the landscape of history a little.

But the landscape I'm creating seems truer today than it did before. The hair salon with its uninviting storefront, the little dead-end street: a storyline was already moving in a certain direction. Of course, the young men were part of the decor. They were probably even some of the key players in the story, but I had never bothered to find out who they were, except for one. Once we made it through the wall, I would try not to think about it anymore. But the uneasiness was real: it was as though no one there, aside from Kimi, cared whether there were customers.

Philippe was at school. It was a lovely day in May, one of those days that make you think summer might finally be coming. Tomorrow, there was the chess tournament, and Philippe wanted to concentrate on his moves, not on the hair tickling the back of his neck like a swarm of small, famished mosquitoes. Days that were different from others were always like a time bomb for him. The anxiety eventually spread to me. It was contagious. No one ever tells you that you can catch madness from children, but you can. Parents have to keep their distance from it, people do say that. The distance that you need to put between you and another person's pain. Pretty certain statements for such an imperfect world.

I left the house and got my bike. Maybe the phone wasn't working. Maybe the salon was closed. I would know soon enough.

Winding through the neighbourhood's oldest streets, I was struck by how tall and green the trees were. I had lived in this neighbourhood as a young girl, and there were no trees back then. As a child, that's how I thought of the city: no trees, no water; plastic animals running along the sidewalks. The noise of planes taking off and landing at Dorval Airport. And the daily clash between the English and the French. The clash had become more complicated. The violence was palpable, child's play no more. The planes still made life miserable in the summer, but the city was divided into two more distinct sections than before: the section for the very poor and the section for the middle class. The nouveau riche were starting to build houses west of the aerospace plant, and to the east ghettos were forming: children of immigrants from the West Indies who had left Côte-des-Neiges to live here.

The salon was in a sort of no man's land: a curving street between the city's two worlds, right near the metro station where it was becoming increasingly dangerous to venture. There was also a clothing store and a small café that played Jamaican music and served smoked carp and crab oil. Kimi had told me about it. I had never been. You had to have good reason to get a haircut at Salon Joli Coif. Or you went there for lack of options, like me. The storefront was practically in ruins, and the tired decor looked like something from the past. Two old hood dryers awaited somewhat dubious-looking customers. Harriet herself sported one of those backcombed do's from the 1960s, her hair dyed a coppery blond. You could picture middle-aged women looking apprehensive under the hairdryers, and Harriet lifting the domes one after the other to check on hair rolled tight in curlers. Thankfully, Kimi was there, smiling, slender, barely five feet tall, hair cut short, amber brown skin, shining green eyes – a real beauty, completely of our time. She was also the only one who spoke decent French in the tiny world of the curving street. The language was losing ground again, particularly in the western part of the island of Montreal. So she was always the one who greeted us, Philippe and me. In fact, I think we were her only French-speaking customers. Harriet worked the next chair and listened without taking part in our conversation – otherwise she stayed in the back of the salon, apparently unavailable. But from what I understood, she and Kimi came from the same region, and it was what had drawn them together in spite of their differences. But Kimi looked as open, young and cheerful as Harriet did disillusioned.

When I got to Rue McDonald, I saw that yellow police tape had been stretched in front of the salon. I leaned my bike against the wall a little further along. I approached, slowly; I was afraid of what I would find, and at the same time I wasn't surprised in the least. The sun was blinding, and to see anything I had to press my face up against the window, using both hands as a visor. The salon was empty. My phone call had probably cut through the silence that appeared to reign inside. It was even duller and greyer than usual in there.

I sat down on the sidewalk. I had to calm down. The street was deserted too. Where were the young men? Maybe they had been selling drugs and were arrested. That would explain why they stood guard in front of the salon, a little mafia basically, connected to a more powerful gang, like the one that ruled the metro station. And the lack of real interest in the hair salon... It was a front of some kind; Kimi mustn't have known, but maybe she had been arrested too.

The local police station was practically next door on the boulevard. Should I go? Would Kimi come out and tell me what had happened?

No matter what had happened, I couldn't go home. Not right away. How could I lie to Philippe if I didn't even have the most meagre of answers when I faced him?

I got up and took a few steps.

Just then, I saw Harriet come around the corner. When she spotted me, she looked down. I wanted to tackle her before she could get away.

But she didn't turn to go; she started to approach.

That's when I first realized that something serious had happened.

Against all expectations, we went into the café together.

I knew it was going to be about Kimi; Harriet wouldn't have been there otherwise, sitting across from me, her hands clamped to her face. But it took her a while to say something.

She lit a cigarette, thinking maybe she could disappear behind the smoke that she was exhaling in short, quick bursts.

And then she mired me in pointless details. It was as if it was more than she could do to put together a single meaningful sentence. I wasn't trying to drag a confession out of her; I just wanted to know what had happened. And finally she told me: Kimi had hanged herself from the ceiling of the salon.

I wasn't prepared for that.

I made her say it again. I needed explanations, and at the same time, I wouldn't listen to them. I pushed away the idea of having foreseen even the outlines of such a tragedy, as if it were my fault, in some dark corner of reality, as if reality were now cloaked in a lie, as if the lie were not being told by Harriet but rather forged by my hearing it.

But it was true.

Two days before, Harriet had found Kimi when she got to work in the morning. She had done it during the night.

I started talking too loudly.

How could a girl who seemed as happy as Kimi take her own life, and in such a sordid way?

Harriet shrugged.

Maybe she thought it was a stupid question, maybe she wanted to spit in my face: is it really better to hang yourself in a chic hotel? That's what I would have said if I were her.

We stayed quiet for a moment, watching one another.

Her face showed no emotion. But her body had lost the struggle. She was hunched and her hands fidgeted under the table.

I thought of Rudi in his hospital room, that little cube in a foreign place, and of the fact that it was always better to die at home.

'The police don't know yet whether it was suicide,' she finally admitted.

Crazy as it sounds, the possibility of murder was almost a relief.

Harriet started to moan.

She wanted to be left alone. By the detective who had questioned her, by me, by everyone else.

I took her arm and squeezed it.

'What detective, Harriet?'

Her expressionless face suddenly seemed drained, and a web of fine lines around her open mouth offered a glimpse of what she would look like older. It was a flash of a miserable future, a possibility that appeared for a quarter of a second. But it did not have to come true. Possibilities lie within us, and sometimes they hijack our facial expressions, like when you inadvertently glance in a store window. I once saw myself old and dour in a restaurant mirror. I saw a darker version of myself, with no way out, mired in hate. With Harriet, the vision was too real to erase completely.

She stopped talking, having nothing more to say.

And then she left the café, leaving me alone, a terror-stricken tourist in a city more hostile than I'd originally thought.

All sorts of things can happen, no matter what road you take, and I never forget it. Death in particular should never be forgotten. Since Rudi's death, I have tried to anticipate and skirt obstacles like an Olympic skier. My imagination is so agile that I glide effortlessly between the little red flags. Philippe's imagination is both infinite and inflexible. It's a dangerous combination. He stays planted on the ground while looking down over reality. Between us, we do a good job of imagining everything that could happen.

I figured I shouldn't tell him the news: your hairdresser hanged herself in her salon.

He got home a little late from school, and I was annoyed, worried; my composure had slipped once more.

'Kimi went back to her country,' I said.

But once the truth is silenced, there is no going back.

'Actually, I don't know what happened, but the salon is closed at any rate.'

Philippe looked at me, incredulous. He must have felt like a small explosion had happened a few hours before.

'Did she leave or not?'

'Yes, she left.'

'What's with you?'

I took his backpack and set it on the kitchen chair.

'What about my hair?' he asked.

For once, I was so happy that he reverted to his obsession that I started to laugh.

'I'll cut it. You know I'm good at things.'

He knows. I can do anything if I put my mind to it. I don't give up until I've exhausted every possibility.

I laid the instruments out on the table: a glass of water, comb, scissors. I took my time, injecting a bit of ceremony into the proceedings. Philippe was getting impatient. I told him to sit down and be still. I spread an old sheet over his shoulders. I started cutting. My heart was racing. I was afraid of making a mistake, so I tried to recreate Kimi's gestures from memory.

'I know how Kimi does it. I've watched her closely. But you have to be as patient with me as you are with her.'

Which was of course impossible. Kimi made everything around her serene.

But I kept moving with her gentleness anyway.

Philippe has very thick hair: it made the job all the harder, but also made it easier to camouflage mistakes. I hurried a little so he wouldn't start to lose his cool, and finally I was done.

I removed the sheet with a theatrical flourish. Like the moment of glory in a bullfight.

'Voilà! The handsomest boy in the world!'

Philippe ran his hand over the back of his neck. He went to look at himself in the entryway mirror. He smiled at me.

'It'll do.'

Then I cleaned up the kitchen while he did his homework.

I needed to save my energy for the after-dinner chess game, but I couldn't get Kimi's smiling face out of my mind. I poured myself a drink, hiding it from Philippe's view. If I could have, I would have locked myself in the bathroom to drink it. Having a glass of wine, then two, and then three… I had come to the conclusion that children see this as an act of weakness. The simple truth is that I have a witness to everything I do. Sometimes I resent Philippe for it.

I had to think some more. A hole had just opened up in my everyday life, and I couldn't help but look through it, even though doing so was dangerous. The implausibility of Kimi's act made continuing on with my day and its series of activities seem almost unbearable. I couldn't believe it was suicide. Kimi's apparent happiness was what we had hung our future on. I hoped someone would call to explain what had really happened. Perhaps I had imagined it all, my conversation with Harriet and all the rest. I had to focus, and I was afraid that Philippe would start talking. There was a fog around me, and I didn't want him to make it any denser – or to lift it, truth be told.

I picked up the phone and dialled the number for the salon. One day, someone would have to penetrate the four greying walls again and answer me. I knew it was an absurd thought. All the same, I had to dial the number and then hang up, like when in a moment of insanity one night you call the person who dumped you. It offers a semblance of proof of existence. And proofs of existence are important. Sometimes they are the only thing that will calm you.

In fact, I was finding proofs of Kimi's existence pretty flimsy now that she was gone. Even the adjective 'dead' seemed unreal alongside her name.

I looked through the papers to see whether they said anything about her. Nothing, anywhere. And nothing in the obituaries, of course. The investigation wasn't over, and the body had to be kept on ice in such cases. So Kimi's body was resting in a morgue, and maybe no one was interested in that body except me. I was exaggerating my own importance, because she did have a fiancé. But I wasn't ready yet for that thought, which led straight to other theories.

The day was still warm, and I went out on the deck to drink my glass of wine. Philippe joined me.

'It's summer,' I said, turning my glass on the table.

'Not yet, gawd!'

He sat across from me.

'You're not cutting any lilacs?'

'Yes, in a minute.'

'Why not now?'

'Tonight, Philippe.'

'Tonight we're playing chess.'

'I can do both.'

'You won't though.'

'You're right, I never keep my promises!'

I pushed a stray strand of his hair back into place. I would have liked to stroke his head until his eyes closed.

'Maybe Kimi's dead.'

'Not everyone dies, Philippe.'

'Of course everyone dies! What are you talking about?' His blue eyes were lit by a small weak flame. 'Except you,' he added mischievously.

'That's right. Everyone dies except me.'

Rudi had the right to die. I even told him to go at the end, but it wouldn't happen that way for me. I had to survive everything. It was oppressive.

But I had picked up the pieces pretty well, I thought.

I poured another drink.

I made dinner, pretending to be cheerful. We ate. Then we shuffled our pieces around the chess board, not exactly prodigies. I was the one making things seem gloomy; I wasn't playing well. My mind was somewhere else. I lost the game, but Philippe took no pride in winning. I was ashamed. So for once, we went out for a bike ride under the stars. It was a good idea. Philippe relaxed, prattling on about the night. Whether he slept or not, he would win the tournament tomorrow. His will was stronger than anything. And I could predict the future, although I didn't say so.

I prepared for the next day, where there was no room for Kimi. This was how I had been getting through the past year, one day at a time. The death of the tiny hairdresser – that's what I had always affectionately called her – changed nothing. At least, that's what I thought that night. Everything had to be visible; I had to see our lives in the rustling of the leaves in the trees; sometimes I had to freeze the frame, a self-awareness strong enough to see Philippe and me back to the present.

He won the tournament. I had his grandparents, aunt and two uncles over for dinner. Tomas and Stefan took turns spinning him in the air, and as usual it scared me. Some men are strangely driven to defy danger, even when there isn't any. Then my sister Christine washed the dishes while my parents snuck a listen at Philippe's chest. Rudi was probably laughing, wherever he was. 'Released' is what they say. I don't know. But in the end, we laughed all the time together, and I didn't see why it shouldn't continue. So I laughed with Rudi in the hallway that led to the bathroom, where I could breathe a little. But my parents' interference still irked me.

Since the great sadness that had befallen our family, every occasion for getting together had to be observed. It was starting to weigh on me. All of these meals had a hidden agenda: to patch a crack. Enjoyment was hardly ever part of it. I had figured out that Philippe felt it too. That day, I would rather have taken him on a trip to Tibet or to a beach in Mexico – anywhere but here.

I kept my secret to myself.

I did what I was supposed to do – serving, reviving the conversation, changing the music – but a scene of desolation lay in the background.

I had become a master in the art of living this way, on two planes. Nobody talked about Rudi. If I didn't mention his name, he was absent from our world. Even Philippe respected this rule. Sometimes I wanted to blow the smokescreen away. But everything was so well choreographed, like how Philippe moved his pieces on the chessboard when he knew he was being watched.

That night, he thanked me.

'For what?'

'For my hair.'

In the dim light of his room, he looked like a small, tired actor.

'You're not talking about your hair, are you?'

'No, but I don't know what to say.'

'That's okay. Sometimes talking is like singing in a storm.'

'Like when you're scared?'

'Exactly.'

'Or when you're sad?'

'That too. A voice can be reassuring.'

'Sing!' he commanded me.

That made me happy. It had been so long since he had asked me to sing.

I started with a Debussy lullaby. I hummed some Brazilian tunes. And then two songs in Creole.

Once I was sure he was asleep, I went down to the kitchen.

It was still early, and I couldn't imagine spending the rest of the evening coming up with scenarios that would just fall apart the next day. I needed to act, and fast. Suddenly it hit me how little I knew about Kimi, and I had to do something to change that.

I decided to call the police station.

I asked to speak to the detective responsible for the investigation at the Salon Joli Coif, Rue McDonald.

I was told he wasn't there, but that if I had information for him, they would let him know.

I thought about Kimi's smile. About her engagement ring with the fake diamond. About her regal bearing even in a shack.

'Yes,' I lied. 'I knew the victim.'

I heard myself say the words as if someone else were talking. Two planes: the song and the stony silence.

They gave me an appointment for the next morning: Inspector Robert Massé would see me.

I had managed to make a first step toward Kimi and her unfathomable death. All signs were pointing me down this secret road.

First I needed to understand where she came from. I had gone to the library that morning and taken out everything I could find about her country, which wasn't much, but it was enough for me.

Kimi grew up in Guyana. She spoke of it with nostalgia. Perhaps because her whole family still lived there. Or perhaps it was me who had read something into her words even though her gestures and her very being emanated a confidence and composure that I found compelling. Regardless, she smiled differently when she talked about her other life, as if she were smiling somewhere else, in a parallel universe. I would listen but all I would hear was the nostalgic sheen of the words, a sheen I wanted to believe, a long way from vast tropical forests, wide muddy rivers, a past forged by slaves and racial conflict.

When I first met her, I thought Guyana was a Caribbean island, a former English colony, like Barbados – a little paradise like that. I was wrong. And she never corrected me.

'I left because of the poverty,' she told me one day, much later.

It was snowing, it was cold out and I was wondering what she was doing here.

A poor island then, like so many others, I thought.

I wasn't thinking. I wasn't paying attention. Not to her past and especially not to my own.

That night, I put an end to my misconceptions.

Guyana is not an island but a country, the only English-speaking country in South America, and as soon as I found it on the map, my perspective changed, the memory came back to me. Not an island, a continent. The feeling of oppression had another source.

The impression Kimi had given me of her country, or the one I chose to retain, was fairly distorted. Guyana is one of the poorest regions in the Western world, it's true, but also – and this she didn't mention – one of the most dangerous. Crime is pervasive, violence a part of daily life: armed robbery, rape and political assassinations. This could not have escaped Kimi.

I could see her smile again, and I was mad at myself for not having asked more questions. She offered me a glimpse of a life that smelled of damp flowers, when an atmosphere fraught with violence was the actual backdrop for her adolescence – a time of life when one's understanding of the world accelerates, a time when Kimi decided to go into exile. It was more than just the poverty that had made her leave.

One of the ideas I had about her was that she was determined. She gave the impression of being sure of herself. But one aspect of her personality intrigued me: a small hesitation, a pause, the tiniest distance between her words and their resonance as she spoke. I often thought that that was exactly where she reached me, in the secret quivering of the air around us.

Reading up on Guyana made me feel like I was partially filling this gap. With what? The beginnings of a landscape. A background of tragedy that stays caught in the throat. Something razor-sharp that moves through cities, both the one where I found myself and Kimi's of her childhood, Georgetown. I understood what connected us.

And that night I knew that, one way or another, she had been killed.

All night, I redrew the geography of her life.

The place they call *the land of many waters* and *the land of six peoples* is not very far from the Caribbean islands, and in the end I had instinctively pictured where Kimi had spent her childhood. It was the West Indies, a place where common roots run through the blend of races: Indian, African and indigenous peoples. The music of the world weaves in through the wooden walls of the houses, the wind kicks up things you can't see, the trees cling to the sky like wooden necklaces around young girls' necks. I could wrap the scene I had created in smells and impressions gathered from my own travels. My night broke down into several living parts roaming the darkness like animals who aren't hungry but who smell food. A kind of chalky dust floated in the room from which I set off to meet the tiny hairdresser. I was familiar with this hot dust, which muted the colours of objects, made the ocean more silent, made time stand a little more still. I crossed the open-air market, running through the rain. I waited in the doorway of a building for the shower to pass. A young girl in uniform was standing across from me, on the other side of the street, near a newsstand, in front of Big Ben, a relic of English colonization: eleven-year-old Kimi had emerged safe and sound from the riot that had broken out between the Blacks and the Indians on the south side of town the night before.

While the president of the Republic of Guyana, Forbes Burnham, was leading his country with an increasingly authoritarian hand, while racial unrest was growing between Afro-Guyanese and Indo-Guyanese, Kimi was growing up in the city of Georgetown. From her great-great-grandparents who had come from India to work the plantations, she had inherited fine features and green eyes outlined with such precision that they looked as though they were permanently made up. Her brown skin came from African ancestors, a lineage that made her a *dougla*, or a *coolie*, depending on who was doing the looking and how they saw her skin. She spoke Creole with her parents, and she was improving her English at school. She was also learning French. She liked French, and her grasp of the language set her apart from the others and gave her a sort of independence, almost a feeling of ease. *Voilà une merveille*, she liked to say as the sun set on the hibiscus behind the house. Her mother and grandmother whispered in the kitchen; it was as if evil spirits had taken hold of them since her cousin's death, and she would have liked to drive them out by burning jacaranda leaves in the hammock on the little veranda. The world around her had become so violent that she couldn't even go to the market without a sense of foreboding. She went out anyway, breaking all the family rules; in any case, soon enough she would be leaving forever. She had said as much to her friend Tamala, whose radio-host father had been assassinated for speaking out in support of the opposition. She had told her cousin John, her little sisters Aria and Lydie, her brother Légende, who knew how to keep a secret when he had to, and finally her parents, who had approved, much to her surprise. Then she told the ghost of her cousin Sattie, who had been raped and strangled, her body found pitching like a log on the shores of the Demerara River.

The country invited tragedy. The words and facts arranged themselves naturally from this idea I had of it. Death herself provided the backdrop to my story. The year Kimi turned eleven was the year of the mass suicide in Jonestown. This was one of the first documents I came across that morning when I entered the word *Guyana* in the library database. I remembered the date – November 18, 1978 – and the days that followed, when we saw images of all the bodies lying next to one another, arms interlaced, most of them facing the ground. It was fourteen years ago; I was seventeen at the time, and it was a tragedy that marked me. And yet, up till now, I had chosen to ignore the fact that the country Kimi came from was also the country where Jim Jones had chosen to build his village in the jungle, where he later ordered the suicide of the members of his cult. That said, at the time, people talked about Jonestown and the commune, not Guyana. The words *mass suicide* were big and bold on the front pages of all the papers, words that wiped out all the rest. But the bodies lying face down did not suggest suicide. No one wants to die face-down in the mud. You would want to be looking up at the sky, wouldn't you? You would want to feel completely free, letting your soul float up to the heavens as the poison starts to numb your limbs. I clearly remember a journalist pointing out a table where you could see vials of tranquilizers, potassium cyanide and cups of grape juice. I remembered the women's clothes, the leader's voice. I have always been sensitive to details: the numbers, the rhythm, the vibration of things. We learned later that 913 cult members were dead; apparently many of them had received an injection between the shoulders or on the back of the arm, and others were killed by bullets and arrows. We learned that they had found preparations for birthday celebrations in some of the houses, that dissident members were brutally assassinated when they tried to escape into the jungle, and so it was almost certain that this had been a mass murder, not a mass suicide. The line between the two is sometimes thin. Regardless, that night, I saw that the two events, Kimi's death and the Jonestown tragedy, belonged to the same slice of reality, a slice where in just a few minutes, years of confusion and lies can rush headlong into the void. This was also intermingled with the death wish that had marred my own entry into adulthood. So Kimi's death may have brought me back to the start of everything. But I wasn't ready to look that far yet.

Hundreds of bodies lying on their stomachs: at that point the image was strong enough for me to taste earth in my mouth again. Young Kimi had no doubt seen the news on television too. She could imagine the lives of all those people held prisoner in the thick, hostile equatorial forest. The rainforest: was that why Jim

Jones had chosen her country? An infernal forest, but virgin, perfect for recreating utopia and indoctrinating followers. Forbes Burnham's authoritarian regime had given Jim Jones permission to settle in the jungle and found a commune there, and not for no reason. Jim Jones was connected to a number of American political figures. Both led a sort of dictatorship of chaos with an iron hand. Lies, weakness and misery were what gave them their hold over people's lives.

Had Kimi, like me, been caught up in the news?

I wanted to think so.

The Guyanese army discovered the bodies that had been rotting in the jungle for three days. Guyanese police officers and soldiers had taken part in searches through the jungle to find the fugitives: perhaps one of her uncles, a cousin, a friend of her father's?

Rumours must have made the rounds of the towns and villages.

No doubt the smell of death hovered for a long time over the dusty earth and near the muddy rivers.

No doubt Kimi had smelled it.

No doubt the cries of the murdered children echoed as far as Georgetown before coming back to disappear completely through the grey roots of the mangrove trees on the coast.

It was almost morning. In a day and a half, Kimi, now dead, was closer to me than she had ever been in life. I knew she wouldn't leave me for a while. If I stayed rooted in the world of facts, they told me that there were over nine hundred victims, and then a single woman hanging from the end of a rope. If I lifted off from reality, I could see Kimi in the schoolyard with the other girls. I could see the unbelieving looks on their faces. And then holding hands to brave the oncoming current, and then something else, and something worse still, and then leaving for the cold country where a better life stamped its feet in the blackened snow. I've always thought you can connect the most disparate of events if you try hard enough, if you find the silver link that joins one motive to another. A chain of events, or of accidents: that's what life is. A charm bracelet that we piece together, sometimes at the end, just when everything has stopped shining.

I heard Philippe moving in his sleep.

He had made such an effort yesterday. His powers of concentration far surpassed those of the other children. It was almost disturbing. It was as if his thoughts alone were moving the pieces on the chessboard. The walls turned into flaming curtains, and the other children simply disappeared. And then they returned. Philippe finally raised his head and smiled at me.

I pushed his bedroom door open to look at him. I couldn't go in; I wasn't allowed. If I could have, I would have lain down next to him. I would have recalled his early childhood, when Rudi was still with us. But I couldn't do that to him, and I closed the door carefully so as not to make a sound, so as not to leave any evidence of my transgression, knowing that he would find evidence, a millimetre opening of the door that would be a topic of discussion tomorrow. I smiled, thinking he was capable of making a mark on the floor, that he would be right at any rate, and that the strongest evidence, as he said, was within me, and then I went back to Kimi.

She had often talked to me about her family – I couldn't imagine her family ties being at the root of such an end. They say the love you receive when you're little and the self-confidence that slowly blooms from it do not fade away. At least that's what I believed. But I also knew that another reality, tucked within the first, was possible. The oppression in her country could have altered her aptitude for happiness. Who knows whether she herself had been a victim of the plague of violence that sometimes ties the living and the dead so tenuously. Maybe she had a secret. Or she was keeping someone else's secret, one that was more than she could bear. She wasn't me, at any rate.

What I knew about her family:

Her brother, Daniel. She called him Légende, because her mother used to say that he had been conceived on a night when the ghost of her grandfather had visited them. Her mother played cards with the dead. This sort of story didn't scare Kimi. *There are many other things to fear in this world*, she sometimes liked to say, smiling her prettiest smile for Philippe. Her father owned a fabric store, and she liked to hang around there with her two sisters, Aria and Lydie. Her mother greeted customers, measured and cut long, colourful swaths of fabric and dispensed advice about making clothes. There were cousins, aunts and uncles: a little community, living in each other's pockets, that she seemed so close to. She was supposed to get married there, after the rainy season, in September, on her birthday.

So, what could have happened to make the desire to hang herself from the ceiling of a run-down hair salon stronger than everything else? Because you need strength, even just physical strength, to hang yourself. And Kimi was so small. So discreet and thoughtful too – she wouldn't have done that sort of thing in a public place.

I knew that suspicion of suicide meant an autopsy. But the police tape had been there for three days. The medical examiner had definitely done his work, so there must be something else. Harriet's demeanour had suggested as much; a reality more complex lay behind what was being portrayed at the hair salon.

I thought of the boys who looked like the salon's security detail. I thought of her upcoming wedding. I knew from the start that something wasn't quite right. Always that smile that slipped out the front door, a shadow that no one saw. And the ring, that fake diamond that she pretended to love. While she was cutting Philippe's hair, I would look at the ring, and it told me that there was no joy in this wedding. Kimi wasn't excited. The day she announced her engagement, her tone was as flat as if she were telling me about a problem with the salon's ventilation. And there was more: a sort of caution strained her eyes, even her choice of words. If I had recognized clear, naked fear, or anxiety, I could have been sure that it was a mistake, that she was lost. Could I have helped her? She had pointed out her fiancé to me, without telling me his name, and only because I asked her, not knowing how to guess which one of the men hanging around in front of the salon it was. It didn't matter, though, because none of them were right for Kimi. I wanted to tell her that. She was going to marry a teenager who looked like a hoodlum. I didn't understand.

I understood even less now. If there had really been any sort of drug dealing going on in the salon, as I had imagined from the start, I didn't see what Kimi's death had to do with it. That said, Guyana was a transit point for drugs heading from South America to North America and Europe, and maybe that offered an inkling as to what had happened.

I had to talk to someone.

The sun came up and Philippe found me at my desk.

'Are you working, Mom?'

His hair was tousled as if he had just woken up from a nightmare. I tried to smooth it, but he sternly pushed my hand away. An infringement of the rule. I turned away to smile.

'Did you sleep?'

'What are you doing?'

His habit of answering my questions with a question annoyed me. It was as if he were always scrutinizing me. And I was certain that he drew conclusions, treating them like pawns on his chessboard. But that morning, I was too tired to insist.

'I'm checking the weather.'

'Are all parents liars like you?' he said, leaving the room.

Philippe was waiting for the day that I would go back to work. He would have liked me to answer yes, that I had returned to real life. But I hadn't touched a thing since Rudi's death. I was a freelance journalist, working for a number of publications, and I had promised everyone I would get back to it. Grief has its limits, I was told. The truth is that I wanted to change occupations. The stories I wrote were hard to take and I had had enough. My last article was about two little girls found frozen to death on a First Nations reserve. The wooden crosses in the cemetery had haunted me many a night. I had seen enough of the horrors people are capable of. Now I dreamed of being a florist or a hotel concierge. I wanted to take care of people without getting too involved, that was the conclusion the psychologist had drawn. He was wrong. It was all just words. Florist, concierge, it sounded good. You have to fill the air around you with calming sounds. I sung for Philippe, I spoke for others. But my silence belonged to Rudi.

I walked Philippe to school. It's a ritual we both enjoy. We talk lightheartedly about important things as we walk. The idea is to communicate without seeming to. Then, as he heads off into the schoolyard, I talk to the other mothers. He knows that I watch him and that we often talk about him. He puts this information in a sort of otherwordly lair, giving it only a tiny bit of importance. Everyone is drawn to Philippe; he is a touching child, but strangely he commands respect like an adult. He feels it, but he takes no pride in it. He sees, he understands, that's all.

'You should become a singer,' he told me that morning.

His tone was mocking, because he knew what he said would have an effect. It would stay with me the rest of the day, like a pleasant companion.

'You look like you just popped out of a jack-in-the-box,' I told him.

I've always loved to sing, which Philippe knows. But I've never really wanted to do it for a living. It was too late to start now. Regardless, music was an important part of my real life, in part because it burned bright in my dream life. That was enough for me. I've always thought that certain passions should remain unexplored, while others, unpredictably, sneak up and wind up monopolizing your attention.

I went home buoyed by the idea of me as a singer. Every day, Philippe gave me gifts like this one, getting right to the heart to plant an amusing tidbit on a part of existence that could have been just a shadow in an awkward tableau. He always put distance between me and the outside world, which to his mind was full of danger.

I cleaned the kitchen and the bedrooms. I had some time to kill before my appointment at the police station. I had to do something, I had to make myself useful. It was still too early to open the door wide to my obsession. The tiny hairdresser watched me at work, smiling. All the windows were open, and it was as if she came in and went back out like a cat in time with the wind.

And yet a sort of excitement was building, as though I had finally found what I was missing to bring me right back down to earth. It was as if I were back at work, but this time nothing was forcing me; on the contrary, something stronger than curiosity or even compassion was driving me. This was actually about me. Didn't the most exciting moments happen this way? In any case, I had always imagined that journalists had to function that way: their own life both on the back burner and in shackles as they go about their work.

Inspector Massé saw me in a small room.

The room was almost empty, which must make most people uncomfortable. It casts suspicion: it makes you feel guilty, even if you haven't been accused of anything. Psychiatrists' offices can have the same effect, for other reasons. A low chair, for example. No matter what move you make, it seems like the wrong one: someone is scrutinizing your every expression through a one-way mirror.

He sat on the other side of the table and opened the folder on the Rue McDonald case.

Up until that point, I could still see Kimi's beauty in life. But that file was about her death. There were probably details about the bruises around her neck, the marks made by the rope, messages on the answering machine, her customer list, all that stuff. Maybe my name was in there. Maybe even Philippe's. Suddenly I wasn't quite as sure of what I was doing.

The detective spoke softly.

He asked me questions, and I answered them as clearly as I could. How long had we been friends? How close were we? Did I know her fiancé?

I tried to overstate my connection to Kimi, and to Harriet, but I didn't do a very good job of it.

It was obvious in how the detective listened: he was patient, like a man who had seen worse, but tension moved along his neck. A tiny part of him had stayed outside the room.

When I got to the end of my lies, I capitulated: it would be better to come clean.

Rudi's death, Philippe, a year spent at half-mast, Kimi's kindness: I told him everything. Maybe it was because of his age and his tone of voice. In just a few minutes, I saw myself from a distance, and it scared me: I had nothing of interest to say, and the last thing I wanted to talk about was my life. And yet here I was, before this man, confiding in him.

When I stopped talking, he asked for my name again and wrote it down. That startled me: now that he knew I wasn't a close friend of Kimi's, or even a very good customer at the salon, truth be told, he was writing down my name anyway. It was information to add to the file. What had I said about myself that warranted such attention?

I had to watch myself, get back to Kimi.

'I don't really believe it,' I told him.

His sharp eyes kept watching me.

'Her death. I mean, her suicide. She was happy. She smiled all the time. And she was getting married.'

He thought for a moment, perhaps searching for the right words.

'You can never tell,' he said. 'Suicide often catches loved ones off-guard. No one expects it.'

He was giving me the standard line.

It occurred to me then that he wanted to keep me at a distance. But if he was sure it was a suicide, why would he be giving me so much time?

I imagined Kimi's body hanging in space. Her legs a bit cold, her high heels overturned on the floor.

I was tired. My sleepless night was starting to catch up with me. I was angry at the police officer.

'And what about her family, her parents?'

'We're taking care of it.'

'I'm sure she wouldn't have done this,' I insisted.

He closed the file and folded his hands on top of it.

Now there was concern in his eyes. That wasn't what I wanted. I wasn't the victim.

'Unfortunately, I can't do anything more for you. There's nothing to lead us to conclude anything but suicide.'

'So why is the tape still up?'

'That's a technical detail.'

He took his time, so as not to offend me.

'Have you told me everything?'

He stood up.

The conversation was at an end.

I was afraid he would find me pathetic. I was flustered: I hadn't even told him my doubts about the fiancé. And all I wanted in that moment was to ask a quick question. Did Kimi leave a note?

I did nothing.

I felt trapped, and I couldn't justify being there any longer. My instinct had led me down this half-lit road, but it wasn't my instinct that was backing off, it was me.

He saw me to the exit.

A gust of warm air surprised us when he opened the door.

I thanked him and left.

Rue McDonald: there was now an invisible border that I would have to cross every time I wanted to go back there. It was like entering a Little Georgetown, I thought. Someone would ask me for my papers. I would be denied access to the country of troubled waters.

It was very pretty, Little Georgetown, but I didn't know what country the other players in the story came from. Anyway, for the time being, the cul de sac was deserted. Even the café had a *Closed* sign. The foreboding the street corner gave off had been taken up a notch. The surrounding emptiness made Kimi's death even more unbelievable. I was in an enclosure where a secret snuffed out people and their surroundings. The secret itself should have long ago lost its lustre. Its violent re-emergence hadn't made it any more brilliant – nor more shameful, which was something at least.

I waited a bit, sitting on the steps of the only little house facing the Salon Joli Coif. I still imagined that a witness was going to hand me a clue. Except there weren't always witnesses, as I knew only too well.

I had to get home for Philippe's lunch. I got on my bike. I was smiling like an actress cycling toward the role of a lifetime. It wasn't natural, but it was nice. Spring, only amplified. Philippe would have enjoyed it. I mean, who has never wanted to be someone else? I would have liked to have been sadder for Kimi, but emotions don't come quickly to me. They get lost in the interval – like Kimi's, I suppose.

But she loved Philippe. I mean, it was obvious. The only reason she didn't throw open her arms when we arrived was out of respect for him. Like a godmother who knows her little man too well.

'Don't you find the name of the salon a little ordinary?' I once asked her.

'I like the word *joli*,' she answered, smiling at Philippe.

'Yes, the word *joli* is pretty,' he said.

Joli Coif. Words were being shortened pretty much everywhere you looked these days, on signs, in newspapers, on restaurant menus – trying to hook you, a trend that grated on me. I don't like wordplay. That name in black letters put me off. In any case, Philippe and I went to Kimi's, not to the Salon Joli Coif. But it was enough to stop me from having my hair cut there: the name, the grim interior, the insidious presence of the delinquents. Another hair salon in the neighbourhood was called Le Scalp. Too good to be true. It made Philippe laugh. Some evenings, with Rudi, we would head out to collect silly names in the neighbourhood. It was amazing what you could find. The three of us would laugh till we cried. Sadly, I've lost some of that sense of fun.

'Where does Kimi live?' Philippe asked when I arrived.

I was five minutes late, long enough for him to have considered the meaning of life on Earth and in other galaxies.

'I have no idea. You know that.'

'You've never been to her place?'

'No, why would I have?'

'Because you're weird.'

He was starting again.

'You're weird too, Philippe, and I don't make a thing of it.'

It was a stupid thing to say, but the harm was done.

'What do you mean, I'm weird? What do I do?'

'You talk to yourself, and you're afraid of diseases.'

'I don't talk to myself, I have conversations with myself. It's not the same thing.'

'So you're two people and there are two voices?'

He hesitated, as if I had set a trap for him, which in a way I had. It's something parents do, and I'm a parent. Fortunately, Philippe doesn't fall for it.

'Yes, that's how you think, with two voices.'

'That's true. You're right, Philippe.'

My boy.

I made lunch and we ate it on the terrace.

'But you're still weirder than usual,' Philippe told me.

He was still trying to get something out of me.

'Do you think the dead can talk?'

Checkmate.

'Can they see us? Do they know everything?'

'Why are you asking?'

'I've been thinking about it.'

'You've been thinking about your dad?'

'Not just him.'

'Who then?'

'No one. Just about being dead. Maybe it's neat. Maybe you know everything! Maybe you can see everything!'

'Or maybe you're just not here anymore.'

'I think they're here.'

'You watch too many movies, Philippe.'

We had started watching old movies from the eighties. The horror movies were our favourites. It was harmless most of the time, but he got really scared when a faceless man came into a bedroom through a window in a B movie. At any rate, every time he watched one he had all sorts of questions. When you think about it, life, death, the long corridor of all the things we know nothing about, are frightening. All the same, the time we spent watching movies together were moments of grace. Our kitten was named Elliott, like the curious little boy in the Spielberg film. A black kitten both reckless and always on alert. We were like our cat, ready to bolt under a chair at the slightest gust of wind and at the same time ready to launch an attack. Curious, but mistrustful.

'We'll talk about it later,' I said.

It was time to go back to school.

I thought about what Philippe had said. *They're here.* It was the plural form that scared me. Rudi sometimes passed his hand between my legs at night. The slightly rancid smell of his hair would suddenly fill the dark of my bedroom. But the idea that more than one dead person lived here, nearby, no. Even Kimi, present though she had been for the past few days, I couldn't sense. How could I have anyway; her body was still trapped in the morgue. To be able to feel the presence of the *others*, they had to scatter into the air like dandelion fluff. It happened long after death. That was how Philippe saw things, at any rate.

Would Kimi go back to her country? Once she was embalmed, or cremated, would they come get her? The mystery would be solved then, and she could float over the land of her childhood. What a joy that would be! Returning to where lies already made everything more beautiful. Returning to the scene of the crime, with no memory of it. For eternity. Unfortunately, death is not what brings us back, it's life, something I was soon going to realize.

I continued my investigation.

The incident still hadn't been reported in the papers. I couldn't figure out why.

I wanted to know whether crimes like this had been committed before. I needed a bridge to the real world.

There was a list of murders of women and children. I had looked at it before. It was macabre, and painfully real. I quickly found what I was looking for. A man had strangled his wife and hanged her to make it look like a suicide. He had neglected the fact that the marks left by strangulation are not the same as those left by a rope. It had occurred here, not far from where I live. These sorts of things happen. They are in the realm of the possible.

A person could also drive someone to suicide. A gun pointed at the wife. Years of manipulation making them feel like they're nothing. That sort of thing happened too. Plenty of deaths from exhaustion and just plain giving up could be added to the list as well.

This reminded me again of the mass suicide at Jonestown.

It took Jim Jones only a few years to convince his followers that they were nothing. But what did we know about their past? They shared a flaw that drove them to this obscene form of obedience.

Most of them were African Americans; Jones lured them in by holding up the possibility of a world without racism, without tyranny. He presented the journey through the Guyanese jungle as a step toward freedom. Forbes Burnham also represented an African minority, Guyanese descendants of slaves who were brought over to work the plantations. But even this so-called communist government used racism to strengthen its grip over the country. Its history was one of domination.

Almost all of Jones's victims, including those who drank the poison of their own accord, had been judged, crushed and then killed. Being forced to drink the poison, to lie face down in the dirt, to kill their own children… I had been trying not to think about it for a long time. Now close-up images were streaming past me and then disappearing like ashes in the wind in the backyard. Past, present and future shook me and shuffled my visions. I wasn't dead, and I hadn't killed anyone. Of course, I had often sought revenge in my mind, for a few milliseconds. I had restaged my own scene with bloodshed. But everyone was party to the massacre; there was no mystery there. Then I went silent, I drank the deadly poison, go along to get along.

Kimi also drank a deadly poison, I was sure of it, as I sat in my cheery kitchen. Her smile was weighed down by a barren reality. There was no love in this reality. Poverty, hope and then redemption: that wasn't the story I was reading. And the end of the story didn't fit with the earlier scenes.

I thought back to the note. If Kimi had killed herself, she would have left a note. I was sure of it. She wouldn't have left the world silently.

I hadn't managed to ask Inspector Massé about it. But no doubt he had checked with Harriet. Maybe she had even found it at the hair salon, at Kimi's station, next to the small bouquet of plastic flowers, or on the counter near the cash.

I had to know. I couldn't help myself. I would wait as long as it took. Harriet would come back. And this time, I would get her to talk. And if I found out there was no note, the fog would lift a little.

Six days after Kimi's death, I found Harriet sitting in the café, staring into space. The yellow tape had been removed.

She tried to ignore me.

I leaned toward her and took her by the shoulders. We were going to have this conversation, whether she liked it or not.

I thought she was drugged; she didn't react. And then, after a moment, she looked at me, and I was able to sit down across from her.

Where to start?

She didn't know any more than I did where the investigation was at. The salon was still closed. She had to find a job. That was what she was thinking about.

I tried to find out who the owner was: 'Was it Kimi's fiancé?'

She shook her head. Her platinum hair didn't move. I thought that it needed to be washed. Ridiculous what comes to mind sometimes. But it could have meant that she had lost control in a way.

I tried to reassure her. The salon would open its doors again soon. She would get back to work.

For the first time, she reacted. How could she go back to a place where her friend had hanged herself?

Were they really friends?

It was a stupid question, and I was in danger of losing her. Who did I think I was? Once again, I had lost my sense of proportion. Sometimes I see life as a laboratory where human actions, even the humans themselves, are subjects for study. I need to understand the animal's behaviour. This may be what has kept me from feeling the knife at my throat.

In any case, our conversation quickly descended into absurdity: I was speaking very approximate English and she quite poor French. Plus I didn't really like her, and she seemed threatened by my behaviour. Perhaps it was my curiosity that scared her. Or maybe I was being unpleasant. It's possible. And it didn't matter. I could no longer make the most basic of efforts in my everyday life. And yet I had worked hard to be able to. But what had happened, which at first glance had nothing to do with me, reminded me of who I was, or rather what I was made of. I was driven by shapeless desires and intentions once again. I didn't know where to go. Sometimes I even forgot my little boy, who shone like the sun, so present, so magical.

I thought it would be a good idea to offer her something to eat. I had to keep her there, keep her from disappearing, which I was sure she would do if I didn't show her some sort of kindness.

She started to sob.

I started talking about Kimi's family. Her brother, her little sisters, all that. It was so calm, so beautiful, so perfect. I told the story I had created for myself, with snatches of memories that Kimi had shared with me. I had to interrupt myself when Harriet suddenly placed her hand on mine.

'Stop!'

What I learned then threw me: I had headed down the wrong path and had to backtrack. I had to go back to the forest where little girls are kidnapped. I had to cut down trees to see more clearly.

Kimi had done a good job of embellishing reality. But what is reality anyway? I had sensed the wings of invention from the start. It wasn't really lying; Kimi didn't lie. Did she invent her story just for me? I would never know. But the wings that gave her shelter protected me as well.

Anyway, it seems that Kimi did have an older brother who was killed by a police officer during a skirmish. A hair-trigger shot, that sort of thing. The police officer wasn't entirely on the up and up, of course. But that's where things remained. He was backed by the henchmen of the powers that be. There's nothing you can do when you're beaten before you start. You have to sit down and grab the last remaining gulp of air. Did I know this? I couldn't answer. Suddenly I felt like it was my little sister who had died. I was getting closer to her. I could see wretched secrets scattering in the sand like frightened crabs. Her soft voice spoke to me as Harriet took small sips of her juice, like a bitter potion served by an adversary. Me, the adversary? She had no idea. She didn't know where evil fed.

If it were my brother who had been killed, would I take up arms? Would I cross the jungle to avenge someone I loved? Would I accept the world order? Would the world order kill me too?

Of course. That was it.

Kimi's dead brother had pushed his family to revolt, and the world order had turned against them. The face of the police officer couldn't be erased, or it was erased just enough to take root under the city's embankments, to appear as a watermark in the images on the front page of the papers. Everyone was guilty, and it wasn't getting better with time.

Lydie and Aria married young, heeding their parents' wishes. They lived in the United States. Kimi had chosen to leave on her own for Canada. She thought it would be easier here, without too many landmarks, in a place completely different from Guyana.

But we often end up in familiar territory. She had wound up in this neighbourhood where, in a way, the things she wanted to forget had happened again. The social and racial disparity. The clans. The secrets that make us who we are. The same little dead-end world. An alleyway leading nowhere.

I now understood why her brother's nickname was Légende. If he was indeed conceived on an evening when the ghost of his grandfather had visited his mother, it was an omen. In any case, he had become the legendary nucleus of the family.

It was time to leave.

What Harriet had told me made my question even more pressing. Had Kimi left a note?

I asked it with great care.

She looked surprised. The idea of a farewell hadn't even crossed her mind.

So there had been no note. Only Kimi's body hanging in the void.

When I left the café, Harriet rushed out to join me on the sidewalk. She held me by the arm. That's when she told me there was a problem with Wilson.

I immediately understood that that was Kimi's fiancé. Who else would she be talking to me about as if I knew him? A pretty heavy guy, bursting out of his clothes. It was him.

Did I smile at Harriet? Maybe I was smiling in spite of myself. I hoped not. Sometimes I do it without realizing, and it's not good. Particularly here, being right would do me no good. All the same, there had to be a guilty party. She didn't like my smile in any case, if there was one, and she stopped talking. I started to realize that you had to be patient with Harriet. The slightest false move shut her down.

I headed off on my bike. My skirt whirled in the wind.

I couldn't wait to get back to Philippe.

I felt like Kimi's story was opening up. I felt like I was going to speak. I felt like I was no longer alone.

The Enemy World

What goes on in the head of a nine-year-old boy? That's what Ana asks herself every night when she tucks me in. She taps her fingers on my temple and then pulls the sheet up and folds it down under my chin as if it were going to stay put until morning in spite of my dreams. She thinks I'm still little and I let her. But in the morning, the bed is a battlefield where I have fought hand to hand with death. I wake up and start to see reality again. I prefer the battle to reality starting over again: my dad dies again, my mom is sad again and I turn back into Philippe with ideas, ideas and more ideas.

I am alive. I watch my mom, Ana, who has one eye on something else and the other eye on me, her son, Philippe. Her secret is kept under a little archway like a statue in a cathedral. Once she cried in front of me, and I brought her the cat. Some snot dripped from her nose, and I don't know why but she wiped it with her hand and then on Elliott's fur. *Mom, why are you doing that?* She burst out laughing: she really didn't know.

I am alive. I control the enemy world. Since May, the threat has been invisible, but my mom is busy again. Sometimes I'd rather call her Ana to stay alert. Ana is busy, and I don't know with what yet. It's like the time she didn't tell me my dad was sick. *What are you doing?* she asked me last night while I was drawing a labyrinth on a piece of paper. *I'm escaping to another world because you're yelling*, I told her. She had just yelled at something. Electrical wires short-circuit in her head and she derails, she once explained to me. It's good, because that's how I know that Ana, my mom, isn't telling me what's going on. Derailing is a word that suits her because she rides her bike everywhere. If she derails, she'll fall of course, unless she's going super fast, like not touching the ground. That doesn't happen, because the streets around here are small and she never goes very far to run errands with her basket on her handlebars, which makes her look like an old little girl. But if it were to happen, my mom on her bike going really fast and derailing, she would end up falling eventually. She would let herself go and then she would fall on the pavement, on the cement, her head split open on a rock in a field.

The day when she didn't tell me my dad was really sick, she found a dead grey mouse under her reading chair outside and she started crying really hard. She was pacing back and forth and then all of a sudden she went to the neighbour's to tell him to come get the mouse. *I can't look at it, I can't look at it*, she said. We put the mouse in a bag, and the neighbour threw it in the garbage at his house. Then, later, she said that we needed to talk. *We need to talk* is not something you want to hear. We talk, we don't talk, that's how it works. If you think about talking, if you give someone warning that you're going to talk, it's because what you won't really say has become too real. So we don't really talk. We fill the void because we have to. *Your father is sick, and he may not get better.* Then it's up to me to deal with it.

The mouse was even deader in the neighbour's garbage than under my mom's chair. This is why I took him back that night and buried him in the yard. I was afraid of catching some crazy disease, a sort of plague you get from miniature decomposing animals, but I overcame my fear to put the mouse where he belonged, here, in our yard. I wore gloves, but I washed my hands raw, even though I know perfectly well that the plague doesn't exist anymore. Bacteria, on the other hand, yes, and you never know what they will come up with. Particularly if you're short on white blood cells. Some viruses enter the body and develop until they touch another body. A doctor has predicted an epidemic of cancer soon. It's already started, I think; otherwise my dad wouldn't be dead. But in his case, it seems it wasn't the bacteria's fault. We don't know why for my dad. But I know that the body has the seeds of this serious disease that sometimes wake up. I would like to be able to see through my skin to see whether my blood is carrying the disease. Ana has told me over and over that it's not hereditary, but I think it is. What does she think a bruise on a leg means? She'll tell me that it's not leukemia once I decide to show it to her. In the meantime, if it gets bigger, that means that I'm practically dead too. It can go on a long time, being practically dead. My dad was practically dead for months and that made us suffer in every way you can think of.

The different ways you can suffer:

There's fear. Fear is terrible and the silence that buries it even more terrible.

There's anger, the fury when I hit my head against my bedroom wall.

Sometimes there's pity, which gives me eyes like an ant.

And then there's sadness, which is sad and lasting.

My dad was so skinny, and his face was so pale, that sometimes I looked at him with my compound ant eyes. A wide vision, shrinking him on a white landscape. Not here. Neither of us. Except my eyes spread apart, trying to disappear off the sides of my head. I was at the other end of the bed near my dad's feet; my mom was sitting on the bed holding his hand, *Rudi, Rudi.* My mom always says names twice. I don't know why. *Rudi, Rudi. Philippe, Philippe.* Except Elliott. She says it once, and then she says *Kitty Kitty.* Maybe it's because he was born a long time after all this. Life changes afterward, but you can't picture how. It takes time to get it, not like when you move and you can't find anything anymore. No, everything is in its place, but nothing is the same. Except that you don't realize it for a long time. Sure, you realize it, but you wonder why there isn't more evidence. The bed is the same, the table is the same. Math and grammar, same.

So I was at the other end of the bed with my ant eyes when he died for real. Summer had just started. The room had gotten bigger again. I ran away into a cornfield like an alien in a sci-fi movie, and then my mom said *Rudi, Rudi,* but it sounded funny. Calm and terrified at the same time. Maybe a horrible calm, the most horrible calm my mom has ever been. I moved closer to my dad and closer to my mom. My mom looked at me and talked to me silently like only she can. She commanded me to take her hand; she softly ordered me to understand what was going on and to raise my defences. She saw that I was a bug caught in a trap in a bedroom. She hugged me but she didn't cry. My eyes got smaller. I touched my dad's body to see, but it was still him, not a body. He looked all right, *he's all right*, my mom said. She had closed his mouth, sweating. And then she called my dad's parents who had come from France to say goodbye. There was a reunion in the hospital room. *You should never have to bury your children*, my grandma said, crying. *He won't be buried*, I said. My mom said, *Philippe, Philippe, it's just an expression.* I waited for her to start crying, but she was smiling like a sad marionette. She didn't cry the whole way home in the taxi. We went into the house. It was silent. We went to bed and slept.

The summer went by, but without me. I noticed the different kinds of wind coming in through the kitchen window. On the best days, the curtains billowed, like sails on a boat. The sea wasn't rough, at least not rough enough for me.

I started playing chess when school started in September.

We adopted Elliott.

For the first time I saw my mom with a cat's face, the face of Ana who doesn't tell you things. I studied her. Her green eyes had new flecks of yellow in them. She was changing.

And I still don't know who she is.

So here's what's been happening since May: my mom has started lying again. If she had thought about it hard enough, she would know that I know that Kimi is dead, not back in her country. She may have actually gone back to her country, but in the hold of an airplane, sent back dead to her parents.

How do I know?

First of all, she cut my hair herself, imitating the way Kimi does it.

That's what she did after my dad died. Before going to bed, she would put on one of his T-shirts and then sit in the place he always sat to watch TV with me. Later, she was herself again, and I was allowed to sleep with her. I would bury my nose in her back and breathe in the smell of my dad all night. It was an imagined smell, because all I could remember was the smell of his sickness, which smelled strong and wordless. I waited for my mom's tears. I was afraid that her tears would build up and one day they would all come pouring out. But I was the one crying.

Another clue that my mom is hiding something from me is that we went for a bike ride after she cut my hair. It was late, I had a tournament the next day and she did it anyway. That's not like her. She wants to put *all the odds in our favour*. She hummed and talked to the stars: not my mom. My mom has both feet planted firmly on the ground. My mom knows how to get out of a tight spot. My mom does what needs to be done. She is proof that life works, even after a catastrophe.

She also said that she's not sure what happened to Kimi: *not sure* means she sort of knows, and sort of knowing is not like her at all. And I know plenty because I went to the salon and I saw it all. Actually, I saw it before her, but I didn't say anything. I thought I would do her a favour, so I went before coming home from school. If I had told her, she would have told me that I don't trust her. Which is true. I don't trust anyone. I trust her more than I trust other people, but still. My idea was to get my hair cut and then come home and surprise her. I have a thing about my hair, which isn't her fault, and I wanted to spare her. Kimi would have understood and she would have said yes, I know it. She loved me.

I'm not stupid. Police tape means there was a serious accident. There was no one around the salon, so I went home.

Then my mom lied to me, and I figured out that the serious accident had happened to Kimi.

She's dead, for sure.

My mom probably thinks I'll relive my dad's death if I find out. Which is why she hasn't told me. But I'm not some stupid kid. Things don't happen as if they're ordained by a great benevolent hand that decides everything. Events, ghosts and aliens don't choose me. Kimi's death didn't choose me. If it chose anyone, it chose Ana. In any case, it has nothing to do with my dad's, which I live through again every night, or practically.

I'm scared, yes. I actually exist through fear. Being scared is important, every animal knows that. Only you have to know how to use it. Before a chess game, my opponent transforms into a faceless enemy. And then I concentrate on a certain point on my body, and I dive in. There is just me and the pieces on the board; there's no opponent.

Ana isn't scared. It's as if the worst has already happened. Her feelings seem as smoothed down as weird hair in an ad. Except when she gets upset, like yesterday, but that doesn't happen too often. She prefers to put her hair in a long braid and gallop around the neighbourhood like a wild pony. *It helps me think*, she tells me. In fact, she yelled yesterday because she needed to concentrate on one thing, and for my mom, for Ana, that's almost impossible. She thinks about Kimi. I'm sure of it. I think about her too.

But there's more.

There's what was already there, before. Even before my dad died. Her flaw. But now, it's as if my mom's flaw has gotten worse. She isn't completely there all the time. That's her flaw. Like a ghost that comes and goes. Like my dad now. And her coming and going in the house like that, if she did it before, it's because she was already a bit sad. She was a little bit gone too, a long time before my dad died.

The nurse said it was good to die. *You know, Philippe, it's a relief to die.* I pushed his hand away because it was getting too heavy on my shoulder. I pushed it as far away as I could. I wanted his arm to disappear out of sight. Just for a second, of course. I don't really wish that people would lose their arms. He looked surprised. He deserved it. I'm like my mom that way. I don't like people touching me for no reason. Most people try to touch me: like an eel, I slip out of their reach really fast. Really, they're the eels. They're disgusting. Nothing scares me more than a black eel wriggling around my bed, trying to touch me. People shouldn't touch other people without knowing what's under their skin. Sometimes it hurts. Bones react. Cartilage and enamel too. It's cold. It freezes your teeth. They should stay away and think about it.

The day of my dad's burial. I don't know why I keep saying that, because he wasn't buried. It's as if I'm learning to talk like other people without wanting to. The day my dad completely disappeared. The day of ashes. Yes, that's it. That day, the day when we threw the ashes in the river, so many people were all over me, a colony of eels winding around my legs. Like I had to talk no matter what, like I had to cry in their arms, like I had to fall on the ground at their feet, some poor little orphan. The ashes flew off in the wind instead of sinking, and I wanted to see everything. I didn't want to lose sight of even a thousandth of a speck of ash in case it was an important part of my dad. His eyes. His black hair. His teeth. So I started running after the ashes that were flying off, and they were impossible to catch, of course, but I didn't care. I didn't care whether it was impossible or not. I didn't care about the evidence. I was a bit lost and I wanted my dad to be whole in the river like a salmon, a walleye, a rainbow trout, in case, you never know, in case he could be fished out, for instance, to enter the world of spirits, of souls, of the dead, I don't know, and that's when everyone got really upset. It was as if they had been waiting for this to happen to be able to let it all out. Arms, and more arms. Sobs. Prying fingers in my hair. Displays of their love for my dad and me. *It's all right*, my aunt, my grandma and my grandpa and all the friends who made up a sort of chorus around them kept saying. Exactly what was all right, I don't know. That my dad was now broken up into little particles? That I had tried but failed to gather them together? That I really believed that his ashes could turn into a fish swimming toward heaven once we left? What did they know anyway about what was going on in my head? At least my mom stood back and smiled. Until she yelled at them to leave me alone.

'Leave him be,' she yelled.

They all looked crestfallen – I like that word – and I took off down the road.

Then it started to rain.

It was a pretty crappy day.

The rain made little holes in the sand with the ashes. It was still nice, my mom said when we went back, just the two of us, before leaving. She had come down the road to get me after seeing the others off.

'Like sand water lilies,' she said.

Of course, she was exaggerating, but I couldn't contradict her. She was hurting enough as it was.

'Why were you smiling?' I asked.

'Because I was watching the scene from a distance, like in a movie. A dramatic comedy, you know?'

That's so her. My mom. Ana. The woman who doesn't cry.

My mom who doesn't cry is here, in front of me.

She lied. I found the book about Kimi's country. She can tell me she was just reading up on it all she likes, but I don't believe her. The country looks nice, with tropical forests, giant tapirs and jaguars with yellow eyes. My mom loves animals. She'll take a picture of an ocelot and send it to me. I'll get a postcard with the picture of my new brother the ocelot. But I won't be happy. She likes danger, she likes the unknown. She won't settle for searching for traces of Kimi in the city. She'll follow the trail, and she'll get lost in the savannah if I don't stop her. I dreamed of the ocelot. There were waterfalls between my mom and me, and I wanted to get to her. But I was alone in the hottest country ever.

She is in front of me, and she is talking to her cat, Elliott.

She thinks he's mine too, but he's not. Here's how I see it: I love him enough, as much as a cat should be loved, just enough, but he's not my cat. While she talks about this and that to her cat, which I would never do, I'm suddenly thinking about her white blood cells. About a disease breaking out in the jungle.

And then I say, 'I know she's dead.'

She doesn't lift her head right away.

'You're waiting for school to be over to tell me. I'm not stupid.'

Elliott lies on his back. He probably thinks that we'll have a long conversation, my mom and I, a conversation that will involve a lot of petting. She rubs his stomach a bit. It's only fair.

'Philippe, Philippe,' she says.

Elliott understands that the petting won't last. He gets back on his feet and leaves, the wild cat.

It's just like the time my dad went into the hospital for good. *He should be able to die here*, she had said on the phone the night before. That time, she was crying. I was in my room, and I heard her crying. She thought I was asleep. My Aunt Christine was on the other end of the line, I'm sure of it. My mom would only cry with her.

'Christine, do something,' she said. 'I can't leave him there.'

A grim voice, full of fear.

I fell asleep. I dreamed about my math test.

And the next day, my mom abandoned my dad at the hospital.

Reality

Philippe was a little bit in love with Kimi. At least, that's what people like to say. They like to imagine a little boy in love. They like to tease to show that they know something he doesn't. But romantic feelings have nothing to do with it, of course. For Philippe, it's a mixture of distraction and curiosity. That was the feeling he appreciated from the beginning. My father had been bugging him for a while about his long hair, but why he decided to get it cut a week after Rudi's death, I couldn't say. I went with him to Rue McDonald. I couldn't have gone any further. He sat down in Kimi's chair without a word. I turned so I wouldn't see my reflection in the mirror, and I cried. Not for long, barely a few seconds. Kimi's eyes met mine, and she turned the chair and spoke to Philippe with a smile.

'Let's bring out those eyes.'

I asked Philippe if I could go outside for a minute. At first he said no. And then, after a few snips of the scissors, he said I could go.

It was early afternoon, the point in the day when I was able to hold it together. Mornings were hard. Evenings were okay: I had a sleeping pill and sleep to look forward to.

We hadn't really left the house yet. I mean, we hadn't seen anyone since Rudi's last night at the hospital. Aside from members of the death trade, of course. But I don't count them because you have nothing to announce to them. I was wondering whether I should tell the hairdresser that Philippe's father had died. Maybe I should explain why we were there, doing something so inconsequential, when we were in so much pain. Philippe had insisted. There was no point anyway, because I could tell when something was really important to him. He doesn't act on a whim. He probably wanted to be different. Maybe he just wanted his head to be tidier, his vision unobstructed. That was probably the reason. Regardless, I understood without needing an explanation. I was there, and it was the first time I had to face someone who didn't know that Rudi was dead.

I turned my face to the sun for a few minutes, and then I went back into the salon to find Philippe now enthroned on the chair, his back straight, as serious as a little old man. A new seriousness, I should say. Not like him. The same concentrated look that I saw on him later when he started playing chess. Except that this wasn't a chess game, and I didn't quite get how the look in his eye and the world had been transformed in ten minutes. I didn't really want to know either; I was just relieved to see him apply himself to something other than sadness for the first time in days.

Now I know he was holding back tears with all his might. Because he had finally been consoled, just a little.

He always gets what he's after.

Brandishing the book on Guyana, he made me admit the truth about Kimi.

'You went through my things?'

For a moment I thought I had thrown him off his game with this lesser truth. His answer brought me straight back to reality.

'Yes, I had to. You don't tell me anything.'

The reality of this upside-down world.

'There is nothing to tell, Philippe.'

He hesitated.

'You want to go after her?'

'Go after her? No, I'm interested in her, that's all. I told you, I thought she had gone back to Guyana.'

'So she's dead?'

'What are you talking about?'

'Say it. I know she's dead.'

I was cornered. I couldn't lie to him anymore.

'Okay, Philippe, yes. I wanted to tell you later. I didn't want you to be in any more pain. I'm sorry.'

– 57 –

He got angry.

'I can't be in any more pain,' he cried.

Then he went and shut himself in his bedroom.

I knew there was no way of getting him out of there for a long while. I didn't try to comfort him. I didn't really know what he needed anyway. Even after Rudi's death, I didn't know. I had learned nothing, it seemed.

I had been evasive, but Philippe's no dummy.

Later, he came into the living room asking me who had killed Kimi.

What made him think she hadn't died of a heart attack or gotten sick? I didn't dare go down that road. It was definitely my attitude that made him suspicious. I was the prime suspect in his case. I was acting like I had something to hide.

'They still don't know what she died of,' I answered.

Which was true, in a way. Sorrow, despair or vengeance could just as easily have killed her. But it was a cagey answer, a trick answer, worse than a lie.

He kicked the sofa, looked at me for a moment like someone who had just been betrayed again, and we stayed that way, another unfinished conversation between us.

Which pushed me to go on. I had a sort of duty toward Philippe now. You can't let death win every time, or let meaninglessness take over. Or maybe I had seized this pretense to meddle in what didn't concern me. A sort of occupational hazard, my job coming back to haunt me.

The worst was having lied by omission again. I hadn't said how Kimi had died. I had left a gaping hole in the story, and Philippe hadn't asked for details, which was uncharacteristic of him. I knew what that meant. If he had the choice between murder or suicide, he would choose murder. Not Kimi. Not her.

In any case, the next morning, I went back to Rue McDonald.

I had read enough mysteries to know that if a murder isn't solved in the first two or three days, the investigation is likely to drag on. Particularly in a case like this: either they find something or they conclude suicide. Basically, doubt is what lets them set the case aside. But who cared about Kimi's fate in all this? Maybe Inspector Massé cared in his own way, but it wasn't enough.

Everything had already changed in Little Georgetown. The feeling of the day after a tragedy had given way to another sort of emptiness. In a way, I was at an impasse again. But a sort of purpose seemed to have taken over the place. The sign for the old salon had already been replaced with a new one with the words *The Edge* written in tall letters. Salon The Edge. The new name grated on me. That's why I hesitated before going in. I was worried I would get upset and pick a fight. I knew I was capable of getting in Kimi's fiancé's face if he was just the slightest bit unpleasant. Hate, even barely visible hate, doesn't fade over time, no matter what anyone says. It hardens. But I had to control myself. Harriet might be there, and she was my only tie to Kimi.

I opened the door, prepared for it all to be new. But I was surprised: it hadn't occurred to me that the inside of a world could stay the same when the outside had new life. But inside and outside don't really exist as categories. Besides, life can never be all that new in my neighbourhood.

Clothes were now displayed on a rack when you walked in. White shirts in clear plastic dust covers, pants and T-shirts on a shelf next to them. The salon space was less well defined. The salon's vocation was less clear than before, if that was possible. There were no customers. Nobody at the cash, either.

I looked up at the heating pipe that crossed the room. I was looking for a mark left by the rope, but the paint was flaked so badly that it was impossible to make out anything definite. Perhaps a body as light as Kimi's doesn't leave a mark. In any case, they hadn't bothered to repaint before opening the new salon. Nobody had felt the need to dim the memory of what had happened here.

It was exactly the same hair salon, apart from the name and the clothing displayed when you came in. It was as if the place had no memory of the event, in spite of the fact that everything was the same, or rather because of that fact; Kimi's death had no importance because the next chapter seemed written in advance. The insensitivity infuriated me. A person had died in this room. Why couldn't you tell? Why had time erased such a strong smell? Why was Rudi's bed remade so soon after he left? Clean sheets were on the bed, people were walking by in the corridor when I came to get his things early in the morning. Already packed in a box. The white sheets smoothed and folded over the green blanket. Normal. Pictures of Philippe and me, cassettes and cassette player in the box. How could I have left them there a whole night? I had forgotten. How could I have then left the ashes all alone for days in the basement of the funeral home? Had I thought there was an urn keeper opening the blinds in the morning to let in a little light while residents awaited the final voyage? Why had the knife not penetrated my lungs? Why had I made it, and not him, Rudi, my love?

I picked up the phone to see if it was working. Of course it was working.

Then I approached Kimi's chair, the first one you would see when you came in. Her little silhouette appeared before me. She turned the chair so I could sit down. Which I did, lifting my long braid to let it fall on her side of the chair back. I needed my split ends trimmed. It wasn't a big job. But she was still going to ask if I wanted to go to the sink, in back, where I could close my eyes and feel the warm water run gently over my head, a few drops run down my neck, and her hands scrub my scalp, or rather my skull, because that's what I felt, the bones of my skull relaxing in the hairdresser's hands.

I pulled open the drawer where combs, curlers, barrettes and magazine clippings were piled on top of one other. Kimi's black album was still there. I had flipped through it once while waiting for Philippe. It contained Kimi's favourite hairstyles, for the most part. She showed me one, perfect for me, she thought. A structured cut, with a little layering on the sides. She would have preferred that to all the perms she still had to do. The smell of the products, the styles from the 1980s, they bored her. But her customers were satisfied, and she smiled at them anyway, maybe wishing to see some younger ones come in, hoping that one day I would say yes. What she liked was cutting hair, not styling it. And I had long hair, but I refused to change. In that I was like all the others.

I found the style she had chosen for me, and I began to wonder whether she might have been right. I pulled my hair into a chignon at the nape of my neck, forgetting for a moment why I was there. I heard her laughing. And then there was a noise, and Harriet appeared behind the bamboo curtain that separated the two rooms.

She stayed in the doorway, unable to hide her displeasure.

I stood.

'Harriet,' I begged her.

But then suddenly someone had me by the arm.

Wilson had just come in and rushed toward me.

'What does she want?' he asked.

I turned toward him and then toward Harriet. So she had talked to him about me.

He let me go, understanding his mistake.

'Kimi,' I called.

I didn't know if I should be afraid. I just wasn't. I was there. I was completely there. Nothing could happen to me.

Harriet said, 'Leave her alone. It's fine.'

Wilson settled in behind the cash. He hung his head, looking defeated. And then, turning back into the boss, the manager of the establishment, he told Harriet she had a customer after lunch.

What was he guilty of? I didn't know. In fact I knew very little about guilt. People talked to me about it all the time, but I didn't feel guilt or shame. I knew when someone was in the wrong. Wilson was. Not me. That's what I told myself. He had changed the name of the salon into what sounded like the title of a bad movie. I thought that the word *edge* was telling. Once through the door of the salon, you belonged to another world – not a world that hides another one, but a world without truth, without appearances. No traces, no flickers of light.

I approached him.

'Tell me what happened.'

It was more an order than a request.

Slowly, Wilson straightened up until he filled the space behind the counter. I wanted to back up. Harriet did.

'Stay out of it,' he said.

'Of what? Did she kill herself or not?'

'Yes, she killed herself.'

Something seemed to prevent him from thinking, but what it was, I didn't know. Not me in any case.

'You don't really look like you're in mourning,' I said.

Bad idea.

He came out from behind the counter, took me by the arm again and dragged me out of the salon.

It hurt. I stood motionless on the sidewalk for a few minutes.

Harriet came to join me and asked me whether I had had enough.

'No,' I said.

It was far from enough. Quite the contrary. My doubts were stronger than ever.

I unlocked my bike and left.

Wilson's attack had awakened another pain. It was a bodily reflex, a muscle memory, at best, because to form an actual memory there needs to be a trace of understanding of events.

I was making myself think about Rudi.

If he had been there, I could have attacked him, I could have pointed a phantom weapon in front of me to stop him in his tracks, I could have defended myself with a stick, a billy club, basically anything that made its presence felt, and then I could have wriggled out of Rudi's embrace and told him I was suffocating, as I so often said in these moments. I would have found my muscle memory, and I would have resisted him, and Rudi would have understood. Stagnant waters have to spill out somewhere from time to time. But Rudi wasn't there, and I had to take care of Philippe, keep him from witnessing this sort of emotion.

I started making supper. Philippe wouldn't be home for another two hours, but he always seemed to get home sooner if I did something practical, something just for him. I hoped he had forgiven me for lying; I hoped he wouldn't be stubborn.

I thought that I should have defended myself. I thought about it with another part of my brain. I chopped the vegetables and cut up the meat; Wilson was strong, but I could have been stronger. I could always be stronger. Kimi hadn't been, that's what was troubling me. Because I had seen her as a woman at peace, and now everything I had built on that assumption had crumbled. I didn't want her to die that way, her body swinging before me just when I dropped my guard. I could feel the weight of her body in the cramped salon. I felt the weight of her body, becoming nameless and changing everything down to the air around me, the world around others, the present and what should be remembered or forgotten.

If I had defended myself, would Wilson have confessed?

There was no love, in any case. No love in that depressing salon, within the four walls where Kimi had announced her engagement to me one day with a smile that already didn't belong to her.

If there had been enough love, she wouldn't be dead. I'm not trying to say that love can save you, nothing of the sort. Love comes as a gift, a gift that you can give yourself if you're not mired in the past, if one of the two people makes sure that the feeling comes with no strings attached.

Rudi was one of those people. I fell in love with him the moment he looked at me with eyes that demanded nothing. I had pushed his hand away and told him all that I would never be. I was only nineteen, a little girl spurning the love of a man with the cold, arrogant assurance of a character in a modern fable. He was alone, a recent immigrant, no family here, not many friends, ten years older than me, and he thought I was funny. And I was funny, almost, perched on a wire of words like a bird ready to take flight. A flap of my wings and I'd be gone.

Philippe arrived two years later like a chick not quite ready to be born. A blue-and-white-striped cap was placed on his head, and I was congratulated for all my hard work. The little sailor turned out to be as robust and headstrong as they come. He had hesitated, but now that he was here, he was all here. His big eyes reflected all of life, all of life.

We were together for nine years, the three of us, under the loving eye of our friends and my parents. That was already a lot, I was told when it all went to pieces. Oh, really? I was lucky? Philippe, Philippe, they're right. Let's thank the heavens for that!

In spite of the turn our meeting had taken, I had a reason to get back in touch with Inspector Massé. He had shut the door on me, but I figured I could try to force it back open.

I was wrong.

Which I understood when he said he would meet me at the café rather than at the station. I showed up anyway, my confidence in my abilities giving way to a sort of fear mixed with curiosity: how would he trip me up this time?

I heard whispers of possible statements in my head. Everything blended with the words of Philippe, who had forgiven me the night before. *I'm not mad anymore. I understand, Mom,* he had said. He was starting to worry about me again. He was watching every move I made. Pretty soon, he would be listening to all my phone conversations, trying to figure out what the person I was talking to was saying. I wouldn't be able to tell my sister or my mother that I was tired without there being consequences. I was wrong just to be sitting here, in a café that was neither a refuge nor entirely neutral territory.

The inspector waited for me to speak.

I started as best I could. Stupidly, maybe: Kimi's fiancé had manhandled me the day before, and I thought he should know about it.

He already knew.

Wilson had gone to the police station straight after the incident. He was one step ahead of me and I didn't understand why.

Was it my fault he hustled me out the door?

Was I asking for it?

The inspector didn't like the way I was putting things.

'Wilson felt like he was being accused. I have to say, your persistence is hard to understand.'

'My persistence? I just wanted him to talk to me about Kimi.'

'He didn't do it, Ana.'

'And you're sure of that?'

'Yes, he has an alibi. And you seem to forget that the finding was suicide.'

He looked me straight in the eye.

'You still think she was murdered?'

'I can't get the idea out of my head.'

'I can see that. I'll say it again: there is nothing to suggest anything other than suicide. No signs of a struggle in the salon. No signs of strangulation, to be precise.'

'Meaning?'

He paused. No doubt he wanted to mark the moment, to get me to admit that I was on the wrong track, to expose my folly to the light of day by laying the harshness of the real world before me. You do that with children as a last resort. It's a treacherous tactic, since most of the time we're trying to show them a world that's a nice place to live.

'Hanging leaves a depression at the base of the neck. If someone had strangled and then hanged her, the depression would be longer. She died asphyxiated, strangled by the rope, if you will.'

I wasn't going to let him play me for a fool. That sort of detail was no more an assurance of the truth than was the waviness of Kimi's hair, or of anyone else's.

'A man strong enough could have hanged her, or forced her. To hang herself, I mean. A form of obedience, resignation.'

'Resignation?'

'Yes, quiet resignation. Acceptance.'

He smiled. Or half smiled, rather, foreshadowing that a case of mistaken identity was about to be cleared up. A window opened on a different side of my personality.

'She's not here anymore, Ana. And her family hasn't asked us to pursue the investigation. Apart from you, no one cares about this case, if I may say so.'

'They claimed the body? She was buried there? In Guyana?'

'She was cremated, and her ashes have been sent there.'

He let me absorb the shock.

Then he said, 'They burn their dead anyway.'

'Who's they?'

'Hindus. Kimaya was of Indian descent, you must have known that. Indians burn their dead. For her family, it's easier to have it done here. But it was still according to their customs.'

'Their customs? Why do you say that?'

'I'm being tactless. I just wanted to let you know that she's back with her family. See, she had a family.'

I refused to understand.

I was shocked, almost offended, to find out that there was nothing left of Kimi. It wasn't a logical reaction. I knew that. I had no say over Kimi's life, even less over her death. Still, her story was unravelling before my eyes now. I was losing something, and I wasn't interested in knowing what. The feeling of loss was already intense enough.

'She was so pretty,' I said.

He was quiet.

'I thought beauty protected people.'

At that moment, I probably looked pathetic, perplexed in any case, because he could have left me there, floundering. But he didn't.

'What are you searching for, Ana?'

He didn't take his eyes off me.

I played my last card.

'You know, there was something funny going on in the salon.'

'I've done my job. The rest is all in your head.'

'All in my head?'

Was it all in my head that Wilson had hustled me out of the salon? Was Kimi's marriage to this half-man all in my head? All in my head, the salon with no customers where he and his associates were probably selling drugs?

I leaned toward him, waiting for an answer that wasn't coming.

'It's a drug thing, isn't it?'

He raised his hand to stop me. I caught a trace of weariness in his eyes.

'Forget about all this,' he said. 'Drugs are pretty common in this part of the city. They have nothing to do with your friend's death.'

'She wasn't my friend.'

I felt like crying now.

'I can't forget it. That's just how it is.'

I wanted him to hold me back, to really talk to me, to unravel my obsession. He lived in the real world.

'I can't help you,' he said.

He was clearly trying to find a way to end our meeting.

Did he want to be rid of me for good?

In the silence that followed, I felt as though it wasn't over, that he knew it too and that I would see him again.

Philippe was waiting for me, sitting on the front stoop. From a distance, I didn't recognize him right away. Well, I recognized him, but from another time. He was a memory. He was frozen as if in a school picture. It was him against a fake background.

He lifted his head and waved at me.

Did he notice my hesitation? I imagine he did, because I always imagine the worst. That quarter of a second when you're afraid of abandoning the person you love most is so cruel – a nanosecond of a subliminal image that makes you think that there is a person inside you who is the opposite of what you are. You would do anything to stop that person from appearing. The same thing happens right before and after death: you laugh at your brother's joke in the middle of the night in the hospital corridor. You drink a litre of wine and talk about a present that is almost past. Sometimes you even feel the rush of being alive, of being even more alive in fighting the desire to die with the other person, and when the person dies, you go on. You abandon the dead to their new state.

I left my bike against the garage door and sat on the steps next to Philippe, my unhappy little boy.

'I have a stomach ache,' he said.

'And they sent you home? Just like that?'

'Yes.'

'Don't you have your key?'

He rummaged through his knapsack and shook his head.

'And what if I wasn't here?'

'You're always here, Mom.'

'Not always, you know.'

I hurried to open the door before he could ask where I had been.

He lay down on the sofa.

It wasn't the first time he had come home from school with an upset stomach. He knew I would go get the blanket and tuck him in. He would sleep a little. And then I would watch a movie with him. We had our habits. Good habits.

Elliott curled up in the hollow of his stomach.

I tried to stroke his head. To stroke my son's head. He pushed my hand away, gently, as he had since Rudi's death. He did it even as a little boy. It was as if he were controlling sensory input; too much touching, too much noise, too much laughter was a threat.

He groaned a little.

'Mom.'

'Wait,' I said.

I went to get the blanket.

I covered him while he looked at me, his eyes dark.

He rested his hand on the cat, who had settled in under the blanket.

I began to pet Elliott.

That way, my caresses would reach Philippe.

He couldn't not know that I loved him. He couldn't not feel it. If he didn't feel it, my life meant nothing.

I stroked Elliott until Philippe told me to leave him alone.

I went to lie down on my bed.

I replayed Rudi's death in slow motion. Philippe and I like two moths knocking against the bedroom walls. The others were talking to us. Philippe answered their questions, paying inordinate attention to the role he was playing. I listened only to Rudi's breathing. The morphine entered his veins one drop at a time; I had asked the doctor to give me some too, out of pity. He didn't laugh. Rudi always said that most people have no sense of humour. He was so right. His death had proven him right.

I feel asleep. Rudi pressed his body against mine. Kimi was watchful in oblivion.

When I woke up, I found Philippe on the sofa, his chess set balancing precariously on his knees.

'I'm playing with Dad,' he said.

'No, Philippe.'

They're here. Hadn't he said that before?

'Don't worry, Mom. I was just trying to figure out how he would have captured my pieces.'

'So, how?'

'I don't know yet.'

'And what about me?'

'You? You're just lucky.'

'Philippe, I'm not lucky. I'm smart!'

'Not as smart as me,' he said, with a lopsided grin.

'That's true.'

He put his game back on the table. The pieces toppled over.

'Anyway, I'm no good,' Philippe said.

I started returning the pieces to their places, bothered by how he never seemed happy with himself, but mostly considering the possibility that he had just lost a game to his father's ghost. We know so little about what goes on in another person's head.

'Stop saying that, Philippe.'

He stood up.

'I feel better,' he said.

I made him soup, and we ate in silence. The pair we formed may have seemed sad to someone secretly observing us. But it wasn't. We were protecting each other's need for solitude. We were very much together, with the cat. The loss we had suffered was not a loss between us. On the contrary, there was a world, our world, where our grief could lay down its head. Monthly appointments with Kimi were part of this world, the morning walk to school, our dinner at the little Italian restaurant on Sundays, Elliott's behaviour, which was the source of endless new observations.

I asked him if he was still hungry, and we emerged from our silence.

'It's almost one year since Dad,' he said.

He was right. In a few days it would be one year.

'No, I mean, Kimi died almost one year since Dad did.'

'That's true.'

'It's weird to think he didn't know her.'

'You think so?'

'Yes.'

'I know what you mean. It's weird because it seems like he still lives with us. He should know who Kimi is. Is that what you mean?'

'Sort of.'

He turned his knife over and over on the table.

'But maybe he knows.'

'How?'

Now I was the one answering a question with a question. I knew perfectly well how.

I got up to do the dishes. The sun streamed in through the window and covered the table in a sudden bloom of yellow flowers. The knife gleamed in Philippe's hand. He looked at his reflection in it.

Suddenly he dropped the knife and opened his eyes wide. Tears beaded on his eyelashes without falling.

'What can I do, Philippe?'

He hung his head and wiped his tears with the bottom of his sweater.

'Let's go outside,' I said. 'It's so nice out.'

We sat in the spring sun, which finally held the promise of summer. Elliott had followed us, and he was rubbing his back on the wood of the deck. He rolled over and let out sharp little meows.

'He's crazy,' Philippe said.

'Cats know how to live. Look at how happy he is.'

'He looks scatterbrained.'

I burst out laughing.

'Where did you get that word?'

'It's an interesting word!'

'Right! I bet you heard it from a teacher.'

'Exactly,' he said.

We talked a bit about school.

Then he agreed to tell me his dream.

'Dad fell off the roof into the garden. I was sitting here, in my chair, and I saw a body fall from the sky. It really scared me.'

'And then?'

'I realized it was him. He was all skinny.'

'Was he dead?'

'No.'

'And then what happened?'

Philippe always told stories very slowly, in fits and starts, as if he weren't sure he wanted the words to come out of him. You had to be patient.

'Philippe, go on.'

'He took my hand and led me.'

'Where?'

'I don't know. To another house that was really crowded. I hate it when there are lots of people around, especially if I don't know them. You know that.'

'I know that. I'm the same way.'

'Dad was weird. I felt bad. He was even skinnier than when he died. I was sort of scared of him too. I asked where you were. He told me you had left. That's it.'

'That's it? Was it a nightmare?'

'Yes.'

'What was the nightmare part?'

'I was scared of Dad. Usually when I dream about him, I feel like he's really there. That it's him.'

'But not this time?'

'No.' He thought for a moment. 'Does that mean he's really dead?'

'Of course, Philippe, yes, he's really dead.'

'You don't get it. I mean, more than dead. Too dead for us to feel him properly.'

'Oh, I see. No, it doesn't mean that. It was a dream. Maybe it means that you miss him.'

'I'm not sure anymore if I miss him.'

'Oh come on, Philippe, you miss him. Your dream and your stomach ache prove it.'

'That's because of you.'

I kept quiet a moment. I was afraid he would bring up the lie again. And I didn't want to talk about Kimi either. We were talking about him, not me and my obsessions.

'And what have I done?'

He smiled pitifully.

'Are you going to go?'

'Where?'

'To Kimi's country?'

'Of course not. Why would I do that?'

'You took out a book on Guyana.'

'Philippe, I told you. I was just trying to find out where she came from. To bring her a little closer. Understand?'

'You won't go to her funeral?'

'Of course not.'

'Has there been one?'

'What?'

'A funeral?'

'I don't know, Philippe.' I wanted the conversation to be over. 'You have to rest,' I said.

His dream was awful, and now I felt like I had put a curse on us. Rudi's body fell on the grass full of holes, and Philippe was holding back tears. My own body was held captive under a rusted metal structure. I saw it all, and I wanted it all to disappear. I had written articles on the unforgiveable things people do, I had pushed these images far from Rudi and Philippe, and then Kimi's pain had appeared like the corpse washed up on the shore. These images followed me – maybe I conjured them, maybe not, but I still had the power to stop them from coming.

I asked Stefan and Tomas to come over. I knew they would distract Philippe. He liked listening to us talk, particularly about our parents. Their peculiarities were an endless source of anecdotes.

Christine came to join us, and we spent the evening chatting about everything and nothing at all.

The anniversary of Rudi's death waited patiently not far from our laughter. The windows were open, and I heard the neighbours busying themselves in their little squares of green. But there was still a bubble of silence that held the moment when I had come home from the hospital with Philippe. The sounds of the world had stopped – not for long, but long enough for the way I saw my surroundings to be forever changed.

I didn't talk about Philippe's dream. My brothers and my sister had been worrying about me for too long. They didn't get that I may be the strongest of the four. How would they have kept going? They hadn't seen what I'd seen. They didn't dream my dreams or Philippe's. They weren't living with ghosts yet.

Philippe fell asleep on the sofa, and when everyone left, I carried him to his room. He put his arm around my neck when I pulled the covers up around him. I remembered the day when I told him that his father had a disease in his blood. He made me say the exact name of the disease, spell it and then write it on a piece of paper: multiple myeloma. Then I had to explain in detail what it did, like a doctor to an unbelieving patient. That's how children are: I had forgotten these details – I would forget them as the days went by – but Philippe, he knows exactly and forever what killed his father.

I tried not to think about Kimi anymore. The duty I thought I had toward Philippe had turned against us. I could see it clearly enough, but I couldn't help myself. As soon as Philippe left for school, Kimi came back with that sense of injustice that always drives me to push things farther. I wanted proof. I wanted to be right. I wanted her to have been murdered. I needed this murder to be completely alive.

For two days, I managed to concentrate on life at home. There were flowers in vases in every room. A rancid odour hovered around us: lilac season was coming to an end, and I took advantage of the last bouquets. The smell reminded me of Rudi's death, and at the same time it projected me into an eternal past, a past where things mark time and make us feel we are where we should be.

On the third morning, I went shopping on Boulevard Décarie. It was nice out, and I would have liked to sit quietly at a café and flip through the paper, but there's no life in that neighbourhood: no bakery, no terrace, no real café. It was as if there were no sky or sun either. I tried to find beauty in the blandness, but I couldn't. The weather was glorious, and yet people were coming and going from stores as if they were in an underground shopping centre, in a rush to get it over with and get back to the car. Who wanted to hang around here, aside from a gang of kids around the metro station? I cursed myself. Why had I come back to live in this quasi suburb? What had I been thinking? What weakness had compelled me? Until I saw Harriet coming out of the bank. A blessing had appeared to interrupt my train of thought. It was a sign: I had to walk in someone else's footsteps. I followed her.

It was early afternoon. I had time, and luck was on my side: Harriet was probably off for the day. She wasn't headed to the salon in any case. She walked along Boulevard de la Côte-Vertu to Belvédère. That's where she went in.

I knew this building. I had spent the night in one of its apartments as a teenager. A girl from my class lived there alone with her mother, an existence much envied by those of us who came from large, more traditional families. She had invited me, and I took a sort of pride in it. But the street noise had kept me awake all night. Dust blew in through the window, and I couldn't wait to leave. I would never have admitted it, but I wondered how she managed to breathe in that square box. Now that the potential for ugliness and impersonality in this type of building had reached its pinnacle, I wondered no more.

The door to the lobby was open, so I went in, and I immediately recognized the chandelier that my younger self had thought demanded a different sort of behaviour. I thought I was entering a more fashionable environment than my own. I was kidding myself. Now I was the one who came from a world where solitude had an acerbic smell, both reassuring and sharp like citrus.

Harriet was already in the elevator; it was a miracle that she didn't spot me.

I went back to look at the names on the board at the entrance. Under the name of Harriet Shadeek, there was a strip of black corrector tape that was starting to peel off. I pulled at the tape, and the name *Kimaya Persaud* appeared.

They had been roommates.

That possibility hadn't even crossed my mind. Nor had I imagined Kimi living in one of the many buildings that lined my neighbourhood. Nothing about this fit with my idea of her, a proud person in a small house of bleached-out wood.

I stared at the board, I stared at the chandelier. I couldn't believe that my Kimi had lived here. I couldn't believe that I was thinking of her as *my Kimi*. I was usurping someone else's world. I was practically in her home, and I was going to keep going. I was pushing into a life that now had a tiny connection with my past. *The past:* I always said the words with an almost studied hatred. So why, at that moment, did that distant connection give me the right to enter Harriet and Kimi's place like that? The familiar chandelier, the worn rug, the smell of disinfectant: I wasn't at home, not at all. But I wasn't a complete stranger either. I thought Harriet needed me. I was being presumptuous. I was looking for clues, I was finding them. I alone could shine a light on the truth. Me, who had let such important things disappear into the shadows.

They lived on the third floor.

I took the stairs. I waited for a moment in front of the door to the apartment. Music was playing softly. I couldn't quite make it out, but I thought I recognized a singer who had been getting a lot of air play. Paula Abdul, a voice like that. The sort of music they played at the salon. Not at my place. I had been listening to Nirvana in a loop since *Nevermind* came out. When I find new music I like, I play it until it becomes part of my DNA. Philippe knew the songs by heart too. Sometimes he danced with me – rare moments when we both completely let go.

I knocked. The music stopped suddenly and the door opened. Harriet ushered me in, as if she were expecting me, and I found myself in the living room. It was a large room furnished in a way that kept you from getting your bearings, as if nothing in the space really existed. The long sofa with a blue and mauve geometric pattern, the floor lamp askew and the window frame cluttered with knick-knacks reflected only the hostility between Harriet and me.

I sat down in the middle of the sofa. For a moment I thought I would disappear: my body would be swallowed up by the furniture, my spirit would remain a prisoner here, finding no rest. And the past would catch up with me, without it being a question of Kimi anymore.

My friend's mother definitely had better taste. I remembered the room bathed in soft pink. I had felt uneasy for no reason. At that age, I didn't yet know what it was to suffocate in a foreign place.

Harriet unfolded a small chair that was sitting unused in a corner of the living room, and she sat facing me. Kimi's ghost would not be joining us. That much was clear. Even if she were looking on from afar, she wouldn't want to put in an appearance.

Why had Harriet's attitude changed? Because I had come to her home? Or was she no longer afraid? Two weeks had passed since Kimi's death, her body had been repatriated, and maybe Harriet needed someone to confide in now.

I'm not fluent in English, but I managed. Her words were punctuated by silence, but not like Philippe: it was as if speaking didn't come naturally to her. But I was used to asking questions and waiting for answers while studying my surroundings. I saw their silhouettes in front of the window, I examined the dusty knick-knacks, I crossed the hallway that led to the bedrooms and I came back to the living room where Harriet was faltering in her words.

I learned that they met through a cousin of Kimi's who lived in Quebec. She knew Harriet and had put Kimi in touch with her. Kimi had learned hairdressing in Georgetown. And *poof*, life could be so simple sometimes: Harriet had hired her for the Salon Joli Coif. She had given her a place to stay at the beginning, and then they decided to move in to this apartment together. Neither of them liked living alone. Especially not Kimi, who missed her family a lot. Luckily there was a small Guyanese community in Ville Saint-Laurent. Kimi soon became part of it. Everyone loved her; that was Kimi. People grew attached to her, tried to discover the secret of her appetite for life, which was both palpable and very wise. People wanted to be like her. Harriet loved her like a little sister. If anyone should have died of something so unnatural, it was Harriet, who had limited talent for life.

And then Wilson had come along. And everything started to change. First the salon. You could feel the indifference, even neglect, down to the walls that had aged all of a sudden. But it was hard to say exactly how. The yellowed linoleum floor and the never-quite-clean smell of residue from hairspray and other styling products: it had been there before but was hidden under a layer of lightness,

Kimi's spirit, Kimi's patience, her predisposition to bring out the best – but little by little the thin varnish of the place had been stripped away. Wilson's friends were always waiting for him on the sidewalk across the street, and there were the others, those who would pass by, stop, come in and then leave. It made people uncomfortable; customers stayed away. They weren't top priority for Wilson anyway, that much was clear. He didn't care about hairdressing, it wasn't a trade that mattered, whereas for Kimi... You had to see the way she talked to people, how she took care of them while she did their hair. I had definitely noticed it with Philippe. She believed that hair said a lot about people's lives, about how they saw themselves. Running your hand through someone's hair was an intimate gesture. You stirred up self-loathing, you turned up strands of hope, you smoothed months of fatigue. Kimi had showed Harriet that. But it was all over, over.

Kimi and Wilson, engaged. Harriet was not pleased. To her mind, Wilson was like a child, not violent or dangerous, just a man-child. That may have been what Kimi liked about him. In any case, she turned a blind eye to his activities. That was Kimi. She had such a maternal way of seeing people. But the day she witnessed a deal, she decided to confront Wilson. Two days later, she was dead.

My conversation with Harriet didn't really tell me anything I didn't already know. She wasn't accusing anyone. She wasn't speculating. She was just telling me how she saw things. That Kimi never should have gone out with Wilson, for example. But I didn't see events as being connected that way. It wasn't a matter of fitting together the pieces of a puzzle. Nor did I believe in the theory of the butterfly's wings, that one thing leads to another, and another, and another; Wilson, drugs, the gloomy engagement. Yes, one small jolt can create an avalanche of reactions. But reality is always the result of many simultaneous jolts. Before Wilson, there was childhood, Guyana, exile. In any case, Kimi was dead, and death always contains a riddle.

I heard the traffic noise growing louder. I knew it was time to go home. But I couldn't bring myself to leave.

Harriet was crying now. She was lonely without her friend. That feeling prevailed over all others.

I stood up.

'Her bedroom?'

She motioned to the door at the end of the hall.

She stayed in her folding chair while I made my way toward the tiny hairdresser.

I opened the door, again opening up a life that wasn't my own. I kept going without quite knowing why. I kept going, just like I did when I dug up what I knew would be a sordid story. But this time sordid was nowhere to be found. It had slipped away like someone with something to be ashamed of.

I'd like to cut your hair, Kimi said softly.

I tied it back with the elastic that I always wore around my wrist. It was something I did when I was getting ready to tackle an important job, something that required my full attention. It's probably why I wear my hair long, to be able to gather it in a single sharp movement, to mark the start of something important.

The bedroom was still furnished as if someone lived there. The double bed was covered with a green-and-gold comforter. On the nightstand was a tulip lamp, a rare bit of kitsch in the decor, and a photo of Kimi smiling in a big winter coat as snowflakes fell. No family photos, no Wilson. Harriet must have put a few things away. Indeed, odds and ends filled the drawer: a nail file, an alarm clock, pencils, loose change. But no family portrait. No picture of her brother, as I had expected to find. Was this because Kimi had erased her past so completely that all that remained was this slightly blurry image of her in the falling snow? I found that hard to believe. Her nostalgia for her country, for her family, was real. I had heard her talk about them often. She wasn't plotting against the past.

Above the dresser hung a landscape that was too wide for the wall; it was as if it wanted to sneak out the window. The lack of symmetry in this part of the bedroom bothered me. I moved closer. It was a blown-up laminated photo of a beach. I thought I recognized the embankment in the distance, but maybe I was imagining it. I tried to move the photo to centre it, but I couldn't.

A piece of Indian fabric in shades of fuchsia covered the top of the dresser, and the curtains in the window were made from the same fabric, a feminine gauze that lent a soft light to a bedroom that was otherwise fairly plain. I pulled back the curtain; the window overlooked Boulevard de la Côte-Vertu. It was grey, dirty, ugly. I understood why Kimi preferred to cover up the window and look somewhere else.

Her clothes were still there, carefully put away in the drawers and the closet. The smell of vanilla wafted out and took me back to my first visit to the salon.

I didn't move anything. What would have been the point? It wasn't a victim's room, Inspector Massé would have said. Plus, Harriet had no doubt looked through Kimi's drawers after we talked about the note. Then she must have put everything back in its place.

There was a cassette player on the floor beside the bed. I remembered that Kimi loved music and hummed a lot. The cassettes were lined up along the wall, in no particular order, featuring groups that I didn't know for the most part, American and Caribbean music. The disorder again surprised me. I had created an image of Kimi, and while this bedroom didn't contradict that image, it didn't quite suit her either. I pressed *play* and rhythmic music filled the room. It made me feel like dancing. I stood to dance a few steps, but Harriet came in, looking annoyed. She took the cassette out of the machine abruptly and put it away in the case under the bed. She knew exactly where things were. It was her disorder I was seeing. Minor disorder, but it seemed out of place in a room with such minimalist furnishings. She must have spent some time in here.

Lying on the bed listening to Kimi's music. Absorbing a little more of her lingering presence. Talking to the ghost.

She calmed down.

'I don't know what to do,' she said.

She was talking about Kimi's things.

'Her family didn't ask for anything?'

'Not yet.'

She sat on the bed.

'Her father,' she began.

She started crying again.

'Her father told me to keep everything if I wanted to.'

'And?'

'I don't want to.'

'And what did her mother say?'

'Her mother didn't want to talk to me. It was as if she held me responsible for something.'

'But what?'

'Not having protected her.'

'Do they think Kimi killed herself?'

'It seems so.'

'Did they ask any questions?'

'Her father asked me if she was smiling.'

'If she was smiling? When she died?'

'I didn't really understand. He wanted to talk about her smile, I think. His favourite thing about his daughter. He was still in shock.'

'He didn't talk about Wilson?'

'He didn't say anything.'

'Not about the wedding either?'

'That's what's weird. No questions about the wedding, as if there had never been a wedding. Maybe that's it, really.'

'What?'

'The wedding, I don't know. Maybe Kimi made it up.'

'Why would she do that?'

'She tended to get carried away.'

'What do you mean?'

'Confusing her dreams with reality.'

'But weren't they supposed to go to Guyana in September?'

'Yes... Well, actually, it was never all that clear. But she really wanted to go back, mainly so her parents could see that she was happy.'

'Was she?'

'I'm not sure anymore.'

So I hadn't really understood anything about Kimi. If confidence in the world was a mask, she didn't wear it the way I wore mine; on her face, it was light makeup, a lie that was even softer than the sound of her voice. I had bought it, and Philippe had too. But I had been wrong. She had no more self-confidence than I did, maybe just a bit more imagination and tenacity.

'If there's a lie being told, you can bet he's in the picture,' I said.

'Who?'

'The supposed fiancé.'

'You want it to be him. I don't know why. But it's not him. They really were engaged. And Wilson would never have hurt Kimi...'

'Are you sure of that?'

'Yes, but there were the drugs... The others, maybe.'

'What about the others?'

'The others could have hurt her.'

'He told you that?'

'He told me to keep my mouth shut.'

'When?'

'The next day. When I found Kimi.'

'And where are the others now?'

She didn't know. She didn't think she would see them again. Wilson had assured her. The salon was clean.

I had my doubts.

But I was no longer sure it was all that important.

'You don't think she killed herself, do you?' I said.

'She wouldn't have wanted me to be the one to find her, I'm sure of that. Why would she have wanted that?'

'Did you tell Inspector Massé that?'

'Yes, but you know how they are.'

I waited a bit before continuing.

'Was she wearing her ring when you found her?'

'Her ring?'

'Yes, was she wearing it?'

'I don't know,' she muttered.

That's when I saw the horror of the scene in her eyes. She was the one who had found her. It was her friend who was hanging from the end of the rope, and I was making her relive it.

'I don't remember,' she said.

She drove the vision away.

'But yes, she must have been.'

She stood up and opened the closet. She pulled out a small grey suitcase that she opened on the bed.

'I did this for her parents,' she said.

She motioned for me to sit down, and she sat a little too close to me. Too close. But I could handle it.

What she wanted to show me was a photo album with a floral cover. There were also two perfume bottles, some jewellery, a few colourful scarves. Opening the suitcase had released a nostalgia not quite fully formed. It was Harriet's, combined with Kimi's nostalgia, now past. It was nostalgia for nostalgia. There was no other way of putting it. People talk about the love of love. It's a feeling you don't experience yourself, but that exists, and even more strongly in this emptiness.

The reality of the bedroom and the suitcase touched me even more. There were walls, space, there was pale yellow sunlight. Kimi could have touched me, stroked my hair, she could have told me what she knew, what she had understood, what she knew about me and my future, and my little boy's future. I had never felt Rudi's presence like that. I thought about it as Harriet opened the album. And I wanted to scream.

It's a scene that I have always played over in my mind: my body letting loose a wild cry before being carried off by a wave. It's not me who's screaming, it's not me who's being carried away. But the scene comes back, an image that allows me to carry on.

This time, I was on top of a mountain. The fall gave me a start.

Harriet laid a hand on my shoulder, confusing my reaction with her own emotion. I moved away from her. She let the album fall on the bed and she left the room. Her disappointment was obvious, but I thought it was uncalled for. I would never get closer to her. I would never pity anyone.

I saw Kimi in the house in Georgetown. I saw her brother, her little sisters, her parents with their arms around each other's waists. I saw Kimaya, eyes raised to her brother. Him towering over the other family members, one head taller, at least. Kimi's big brother. I saw a church. I saw a trip to the market. I saw the brother revered, and then absent. I saw the colours, the landscape. I saw a greyness that you don't find in a hot city: Kimi's eyes already reflecting a different world. Snow on Kimi's hair. I saw Kimi leave, I saw her alone in the crescent of the street. And then I saw myself escaping from the dead-end too.

I put the photo album back in the suitcase.

Harriet was waiting in the kitchenette now. She had made coffee. I didn't want any.

I didn't know what I was looking for anymore. But I wasn't going to find anything here but evidence of life, and in spite of the sadness, no argument for, or against, death.

I hadn't really dreamed in a long time. Philippe was the one who stayed connected to the world where the dead are supposed to reconcile themselves with their lives. And with ours, of course. Rudi had often come to visit him, but recently his visits were more like nightmares. He pulled a string in the yard to lure Philippe toward the shadows, as if attracting a feral cat. I wanted him to leave him alone, but how do you plead with a dead person? How do you ask him to get out of the head of a nine-year-old boy?

Rudi had taken the cat with him. He had tied him to a tree, and Philippe started to scream. *You'll kill him*, he was yelling when I went into his bedroom. The rope was around the cat's neck, and Philippe knew that he would try to get away and end up strangling himself.

'Cats won't be kept prisoner,' he said.

'It's the anniversary,' he said a second later, his big grey-blue eyes still scared.

Suddenly they were Rudi's eyes on the day of his death.

And then they weren't.

They were Philippe's eyes, on the morning of the anniversary of his father's death.

They were calling me to order, and I still hadn't planned anything, disloyal person that I am.

Proof

The white blood cells are the main enemy. If I had an instrument to count them, I would. I would gently insert it under my mom's skin while she was sleeping, I would point it toward the marrow of each of her bones and then I would know whether her white blood cells were decreasing or increasing. I would see whether they had invaded my mom's blood, whether they were multiplying like invisible, poisonous mushrooms underground on the roots of a tree. This could be because of a whole bunch of diseases. But my dad's disease is the worst, that's for sure.

My mom says you can't catch leukemia. She says it again and again, and what she says goes over my head like a flock of sparrows. Okay, it's reassuring. But it doesn't last. She also says, not to me, but to my grandma or Christine, she says that doctors don't know anything. I have my doubts too. I'm like her, and I don't see why white mushrooms couldn't pass from one body to another. Anyway, every disease is around us, here, in the air, and I don't want to catch one. Just thinking about it makes me want to forget about everything. I could forget about school. I could stop making an effort to work or to do anything. I would forget to feed the cat. I would forget to breathe. I don't say this to my mom. But she thinks like me. She could forget about everything too. Except the cat, in her case. And me, of course.

So far, she still comes to meet me every day after school. She smiles a lot, like the other mothers. She smiles, she talks, she makes faces, she dances in place. But even from far away, you can tell that she's different. You can see it. It's her, that's all. The others blend into the group of mothers waiting for their kids. They are like a landscape, and you can't pick out the details unless my mom is there. She's the detail, Ana. A mom who is also a stranger to me.

She puts her hair in a long braid and comes to wait for me at the corner, stamping her feet. She talks to the animals she meets along the way. *Look at that, Philippe,* she says. When she laughs with her hands on her cheeks, it's a cat. Cats are cute, dogs are pitiful: that's the way she sees things. At night, she watches me doing my homework and then she asks me whether I want to play chess. I almost always say no. She doesn't get why. I explain: in chess, one false move and it's all over. You have to think, think and wait, and remember. My mom is impatient, which is not good. She has to move, no matter what. That's why I don't play with her that often. It may be partly my fault, but she'll never be good at chess. My dad would have been, but he's not here anymore. I won't tell my mom right away. But he's really not here anymore.

Twice in one week, she wasn't there either when school got out. No braid spinning in the air when she moves. It had never happened before.

The first time, I had the crazy idea that she had abandoned me to the enemy. She had already told her sister that she couldn't *do this for anyone else.* So that was it: she knew I was sick, she had noticed the bruise on my thigh, and she didn't want to admit it to me because she knew that she couldn't *do this* for me. Take care of me while I was sick. She would abandon me, leave me with someone else, maybe Kimi? But then Kimi died all of a sudden. Maybe that was why it upset Ana so much. It upset her plans, and she was looking for someone else. So maybe I should leave, leave the house and the cat. I would have to speak another language. And I couldn't talk to anyone about my dad anymore.

She came back.

So the second time, I knew that she was the one battling with him. The other enemy, the one I don't know. My thoughts got tangled up like my mom's doodles when she spends hours on the phone, drawing little arrows on a piece of paper.

I can go home alone. I went home alone. But worry gnawed at my stomach.

Where was my mom?

Why was she pulling away from me like this?

Ever since we had been on our own, at least there was that: she was with me 100 percent. But not now.

'School's almost over,' I said when she came into the kitchen.

She didn't understand.

'It's exams. I'll be home earlier and earlier,' I said.

She sat down, looking tired.

'I went shopping.'

'Where are the bags?'

There were no grocery bags or anything.

She shook her head, discouraged with me.

'What are you investigating?' she asked.

I didn't answer. I was investigating her and she knew it.

I went back to what I was doing. I got up on a chair to put sardines on top of the fridge.

'What are you doing?' she asked.

Finally she was waking up.

My mom gives the cat sardines as a reward, but I think we should recreate life in the wild.

'He needs to hunt for his food,' I said.

'Who?'

'Elliott, jeez.'

She let me be. My mom never interferes when I'm experimenting.

She still looked mad, but not at me. Disappointed maybe. In conversation with someone other than me.

Elliott came in meowing.

This took our mind off things. We watched him search.

It only took a minute before he was perched on the fridge.

'Wow! Way to go!' I said.

My mom started to laugh: 'You're making fun!'

The cat ate it all and then licked his paws.

I actually like him quite a lot.

In the evening, we made a special dinner. It was the anniversary of my dad's death. The river where his ashes floated was in the Gaspé, a nine-hour drive from here. I would have liked to have gone, but my mom said later, this summer.

It wasn't a real ceremony: she hadn't invited anybody.

The phone rang a thousand times, and she spoke in her hushed voice. She didn't have much to say.

She likes to talk about everything. She talks to the cashier at Provigo about me, she laughs with the neighbour who takes in stray cats. That's actually the only reason she talks to him, to get news about the little cats that she sometimes picks up in the yard. She told our other neighbour all about Rudi getting sick. But I haven't heard her talk about our hairdresser yet. To anybody. This is how I know that her death is an even more terrible secret.

We ate my dad's favourite fruit pie. I didn't get why.

She said, 'It's to remember him.'

I remember him without the pie. And he couldn't have a piece.

When I couldn't hold back anymore, I told her, 'You know, Kimi didn't let me cry.'

Then she made me tell her how Kimi had stopped me from crying the first time. My tears caught in a trap of words like fish in a net. One—nothing for me. Too bad, tears.

It didn't last long.

I wanted with all my might to think about my dad. So that he wouldn't be alone.

I wanted fun memories. Me with long hair, and my dad in his leather jacket that smells like a walk in the woods. But again I went back to the memory of the days where it all skidded toward my dad's death.

'We'll go to the Gaspé this summer,' my mom said again.

She was trying to stop my tears.

'I'll rent a house,' she said.

Words, words, words.

I nodded my head like an old child who doesn't believe his mom.

The candles made everything in the dining room look dramatic.

She talked about Rudi. She said how much he loved us, how he loved nature, how he was different from her, but the same too.

Different: him, patient and slow like a bear; her, watchful and fast like a deer that appears suddenly on the side of the highway.

Same: they like planning trips they won't take, they read newspapers for hours, they go out without me but come home early because they missed me too much, they'd say, laughing. They laugh a lot. A lot.

Different: sometimes it's as though my mom's laugh is too weak, as if she gave up on it somewhere along the way.

But maybe I made this up when I saw my dad comforting her in the dark. It happened a long time ago, but it feels like yesterday in my head. It was when all of a sudden everything changed for days, like when there's a car accident or a fire or maybe when war is declared. My mom had made an urgent call to him when she came home. I was little, but I knew something was going on. Little, but not stupid. My grandma was taking care of me, and my mom came in and told her to go home. She never says things like that. My grandma did what she was told. She said she would come back later. *I have to deal with something*, my mom said, sort of apologizing. Were they arguing? When my dad came home, they went up to their bedroom without saying a word, without even noticing I was there, but I followed them, like a shadow, and I saw my mom crying in my dad's arms. Later, a policeman rang the doorbell. I was the one who opened it. My dad's mistake, he admitted to me later. The policeman had come to take a statement. That was the word I heard. My mom's *statement*. I didn't care about words at the time, but I cared about the policeman in his uniform sitting in the kitchen across from my mom who was holding my dad's hand. This is probably why the word is stuck in my mind and keeps flashing on my list of unanswered questions. The policeman was wearing a big belt that had a walkie-talkie attached to it that made noises with mysterious, complicated powers. I felt like it was complicated. He was asking questions, and my mom was answering like a good student holding her guardian angel's hand. I could see all this from a distance. I was on the staircase. It was serious. My mom's voice would get louder and then get muffled. They had forgotten all about me.

The policeman left, and my parents were silent for a long time in the kitchen. The next few hours were filled with hard minutes like rocks pelting the roof of the house. Until they decided to send me to spend a few days at my grandma's. *Your mother's tired*, my dad said. That's what she said about my dad too when he first started to get sick. *Your mother saw a bad man*, he had to add when he saw my anxious little face. *She's brave, you see, she told the police about it*, he said.

'Is she going to leave?' I asked.

That's not what I wanted to say. I probably wanted to say the word *die*. I wanted to say *we*. *Are we going to leave?* Now that there was a threat in the house. Ana, my mom, was kicking the wall and saying she shouldn't have come back here. Later, when my dad died, I thought that something had exploded, that nothing worse could happen. But the threat is still here.

My dad took me in the car with him.

When I came back from my grandma's, everything was like before, or almost. I was little, but I remember my mom being too calm. Or I imagine that I remember. I have to remember. To understand what's happening now. Is it all connected? At three years old, coming home from my grandma's, afraid of change, afraid of a bad man, my mom talking to the policeman, her pale skin almost blue in the daylight, then the whispers, the silence filled with screaming, and then my dad's slow death like a butterfly being snuffed out, and now Kimi's death, the police tape, and my mom full of secrets again and then forgetting to prepare a ceremony for my dad?

I threw my pie in the garbage.

'Philippe, Philippe,' my mom said.

I looked her straight in the eye this time.

Long silence.

And then: 'It's true, he's here,' she said.

She really would do anything for me, even lie to herself.

That's why my proof is always her lies.

She is sleeping on the sofa and doesn't believe in ghosts.

In her purse, she has her wallet, her sunglasses and receipts from the grocery store, the dépanneur and the pharmacy. I open her wallet and see the picture of my dad through the little see-through plastic window, always in its place. Mine is in the window across from it. I'm seven and I'm standing in front of a tree, smiling. I look through the wallet, nothing. I look through the pockets, nothing.

I go up to her bedroom and look through her drawers. My dad watches me, disapproving, but I keep going. The cat stands watch in the doorway, my mom's protector, but I keep going.

Her clothes are in messy piles as if she never cleans up. Her clothes are colourful and don't say anything about her. I don't understand why my mom likes bright colours and mess so much. There's a pile of books beside her bed. I flip through each book to see if there's a clue to why my mom is sad. I open her desk drawer and look through her papers. My mom is still my mom, and I don't understand where the other mother, Ana, is. There's a notebook, but the notes were taken before my dad died, when she was working. I know that because she wrote dates in it.

My dad tells me gently to close the drawer, to stop all this. I listen because I feel bad. And then I feel a hand on my shoulder. It's my mom. Wide awake.

She grabs me and holds me by the arms, tight. She shakes me a little.

'Why are you doing this?' she says. 'Why don't you ever leave me alone? Why is this happening to me?'

The whys keep coming.

She shakes me again. I don't fight back. I'm sure I'm stronger than her. Even as she's shaking me, she seems small and fragile.

She stops all of a sudden and falls into her chair. What have I done to her? She's out of breath. I'm afraid for her, but I run out of the bedroom. I'm too afraid of her dying. I'm afraid she'll disappear in front of me, that she'll evaporate, that she'll go out like the flame of a candle when the door opens and the party is over.

She joins me later, and we read a book together as if nothing happened.

'I'll never leave you alone,' she says as I'm drifting off to sleep.

Maybe not.

Maybe I made it all up.

But the next day, a policeman rings our doorbell again, like when I was three years old, and I'm the one who answers the door again, and once again my mom is advancing toward an enemy I don't know.

Statements

None of the women were allowed to use the name Linda ever since a woman named Linda had deserted.

I suddenly remembered that detail while Inspector Massé was talking to me. Sharon Amos had been one of them. She had managed the headquarters in Georgetown. When she knew that the end had come, she slit her three children's throats with a kitchen knife. Then she asked someone to slit her throat. Had she been found at the same time as the others in the jungle? I don't know. In fact, even at the time, it wasn't clear to me. It wasn't clear to anyone. The accounts were too absurd to be taken individually. The words were twisted like the bodies, face down on the ground; it was impossible to turn them over and grasp the exact meaning of what they were saying. On the one hand, there was everything that had been poisoned – the words, life, the bodies piled three or four deep – and on the other, but not completely on the other, because the voice kept speaking over the images, the madness of the man everyone called Dad. Dad would have been proud of the woman no longer named Linda who had slit her three children's throats, unless I'm confusing the Lindas, and Sharon Amos was someone else, one of his favourites, who wanted to do what he asked her to do but whose body rebelled at the last minute. In any case, I remembered this sentence clearly: *Dad would have been proud.* Someone had said it. He told them that they had to die for the revolution. He crushed them and then he killed them.

I had watched the events from my bed. We had turned on the TV in my hospital room, I imagine because they thought that my days were too long. But that's not how it was. The days were nothing, and the mass suicide filled them with an even greater horror than the one I had just been through. I didn't know if it was helping me. It was what it was, that's all. My eyes were seeing the world as it was.

So the inspector came back. While he was talking, I was thinking back to that woman who had changed her name. What is a name after all? What is a life? And time, what is time if Kimi's death was bringing me back to the end of an adolescence that had been seared with a brand?

I didn't pay attention to the name of Kimi's country the one time she mentioned it, because I had already buried the sound of it under many other noises. I was appalled by that now, ashamed as if I had given a false statement to Inspector Massé, as if part of me had kept my eyes closed, wasn't lucid or intelligent, and I despised this part of me.

Philippe was sitting in the kitchen, and I knew he was listening to my conversation with Robert Massé, but I didn't have the energy to get up and tell him to go play somewhere else. Would he have done it? Of course not. I was thinking about the thing about first names. I was letting that sort of detail take over my brain. The taste of earth in my mouth. The softness of the blanket they wrapped around me in the ambulance. How the cold came through the window that was slightly ajar in my hospital room, how I insisted that the nurse leave it open. The white shirt of the detective sitting before me.

'It's a policeman without a uniform,' Philippe had warned me.

'So how do you know it's a policeman?'

'He told me.'

I never know what he's really thinking.

Except this time.

He told me this in an assertive tone, as if to shut me up, to show me that he remembered something, even if he didn't understand everything. The past came flooding back: my little baby curious and worried in front of the police officer, my little boy silent and frightened.

He was right to warn me.

Because now, in spite of the warning, the whiteness of the shirt of the man before me was confusing me. He had supposedly come to tell me that Wilson and the other guys had been arrested for drug trafficking and that the salon was closed. That there would be a trial.

But once he had said it, he didn't move.

'Why did you come to tell me that?'

It was hot; the sun was streaming in though the living room window. I could feel sweat starting to trickle down my neck. I was dressed sloppily, in clothes you wear around the house. All I could think of was going upstairs to change. But you can't really do that. Anyway, every time I put on a dress, Philippe looks at me as if I were someone else, as if I were going to trade in my life and abandon him. The detective would have to put up with me like this.

'Your affection for Miss Kimaya.'

'But what does this change for her?'

'I thought you would want to know, that's all.'

And yet he stayed where he was.

'And Harriet?'

'We spoke to her this morning. She's already found a job in another salon.'

'Where?'

'In Cartierville.'

'Is she in any danger?'

'No, I don't think so, really. She never said anything. And they're small-time dealers, you know.'

It was small talk. I really didn't care about Harriet and he knew it.

'You play chess?' he asked.

He was trying to soften me up.

'No, my son, Philippe, does.'

'He must be smart,' he said.

He smiled. I didn't. I wanted him to leave.

But it was as if he had all the time in the world.

He picked up a piece from the chessboard and twirled it between his fingers.

I heard Philippe throw the ball for the the cat in the kitchen. He was probably trying to get him out from under the table. Elliott the feral cat. Pretty soon he was going to crouch and wiggle, preparing to bolt across the hallway and race up the stairs. It was his own little war. Once upstairs, he could choose any hiding place he liked to lie down and stretch out his full length. Feline calm. I hoped Philippe would follow him.

'I was wondering...' Robert Massé said.

He was being too hesitant.

'I was wondering why you came to see me, really why, and why you were so insistent.'

'For Kimi, I told you. I was trying to piece her story together, a sort of funereal tribute, if you will. I feel like I owe it to her. It may not even be as personal as that. I mean, investigating is sort of what I do.'

'I know. I've read a few of your articles. They're good.'

'Tough stories. I'm going to change fields.'

'I understand.'

He was searching for a way to broach the subject. He jumped in.

'You seemed so tormented, I thought there was something else connecting you to your hairdresser.'

He let the silence hang in the air for a moment, as if he were hesitating again. He was heading into dangerous territory, where his curiosity was the main suspect. I took the queen from his hand and placed it back on the chessboard. If he had something to say to me, he would have to do it without a crutch.

'So you believed me at the start?'

'You know, in an investigation, everything is important, although not everything is immediately significant: they're objects, words and movements that line up like numbers in an equation on a blackboard. You just have to be able to spot them fairly fast. Then it's not too hard to follow a lead, to find what you're looking for. The question is always knowing whether things are connected, and if they are, how.'

'And you found that connection between me and Kimi?'

'In a sense, yes.'

He said yes while shaking his head. It wasn't what he really wanted to talk about. I highly doubted it.

'Well, actually, I remembered your name,' he said.

That's when I started thinking about the girls named Linda. Maybe I should have changed my name too. My name, a little planet blinking on his blackboard, had led him here, to my house, today. And I didn't want to remember.

He kept advancing as I moved further away.

'I was at the same station fourteen years ago. You don't forget that sort of thing. You always hope you'll find what's missing to tie up the loose ends.'

'I don't want to talk about that,' I said.

'I think you do.'

He had some nerve saying that. But his tone was so confident that I didn't even try to defend myself. He was right: I couldn't escape it any longer.

I got up to see what Philippe was doing in the kitchen.

'Is the policeman nice?' he asked.

'Yes, Philippe, very nice.'

'You're lying.'

I bent under the table to pet Elliott. After a moment, I managed to pick him up.

Philippe opened the door. The cat jumped to the ground and went out.

'Can you go outside too?' I asked.

I sounded too casual. Philippe wasn't fooled.

'Why?'

'Because I'd like to talk to Inspector Massé.'

He didn't move.

'You can talk,' he said.

'Go outside,' I said.

'But you can talk with me here!' Philippe cried.

I imagined the reaction of the man sitting in the living room. I hoped he felt as bad as I did. At the same time, I didn't want him to think anything at all about my son, or my relationship with him. People tend to rush to judgment about mothers, about how they are with their children and about the children themselves. They like to think they would have done better, and that we had done too much. I have often had a taste of this medicine. Illness and grief are the best barometers for what people really think. What they think of themselves, in fact.

Once again I found myself torn between two options: the one where I was finally serene, fulfilled, with my little boy, and the one where I was me, Ana, the woman who would do anything for a moment without a witness, a moment to be completely herself, alone, wounded, solid, planted in the present like a strong tree in a devastated village.

'Philippe,' I said, 'Philippe, please.'

'Is this about Dad? Or you?'

He was terror stricken again. It was my fault. I didn't know how to present reality devoid of its contents without making him suspicious. I was trying to deal with this character flaw. All these years I had been trying. Every time I got that sense of disaster or terrible news awaiting me if I was too far from home, from my nest, I tried to push it away. The worst had already happened, I kept telling myself. But Rudi had been there to protect us, and I had to accept his death: the premonition kept coming back. I had to live with it.

'Of course not, Philippe, why would he be talking to me about Dad?' I said, pretending to find the idea funny.

'What did he do?'

'Who?'

'Dad.'

'Nothing, come on, I don't know what you're imagining. He came to talk to me about Kimi.'

I took him by the hand.

'Come on,' I said. 'We'll go ask him.'

He followed me into the living room and let go of my hand upon seeing Inspector Massé. We sat on the sofa in front of him.

I said, sharply, 'So, you were saying, Mr. Massé, the salon is going to close?'

He had to play along.

'Yes, there's no one left to run it.' He thought before adding, 'We arrested the bad guys.'

'I'm not stupid,' Philippe mumbled.

The inspector looked at me, caught in a gaffe.

I sighed. He was going to have to figure this one out on his own.

'Okay. It was a minor drug thing. Your mother will explain it all later.'

'But Kimi?'

'She must have been very sad to do what she did.'

I immediately wanted to put this gaffe right, but Philippe bravely acquiesced, and I stayed quiet.

He turned toward me. He pursed his lips.

The two of us were separated by our thoughts.

Then a surreal scene followed: the inspector talking chess strategy with my son.

They had forgotten I was there.

In the meantime, I was preparing to answer the questions. As I had done fourteen years before, sitting in my parents' living room, and then at the hospital. And eight years later, right here, in the kitchen.

I wasn't called Linda. Or Ana.

At that moment, lying on my stomach under the swing that must have stopped moving because I no longer heard the squeaking, at that moment my name was nothing, my name was the sound at the end of the squeaking, the sound of the voice of the boy a little older than me who was breathing like one human being too many on this earth. Not an animal, no, a human being, the human being who had just shown me the chords for a Doors song on the guitar, 'Love Street.' I could still hear the melody, but it was fading away. I wanted it to fade away. I wanted to unravel the chaos and hear the sound of reality, what was happening, here. Was it happening? Had the boy already beaten and raped someone else? Then I should have known. Was it bad luck? Was it ignorance? I was asking myself that, I was telling myself that, *I am being beaten, my name is I am beaten, my name is I am raped*, my face pressed into the cold ground in the deserted park, my cheek hurts because there is a rock just under my eye, under my cheekbone, I'm going to move, I have to, I have to move a little if I don't want to get hurt. And where was everyone, anyway? Was it a part of a plan? Of course, in the fall there's no one in the park, I thought, and the pool is empty. He could have thrown me in the empty pool, killed me faster than this, it would have been much better to crash onto the turquoise cement, I thought, but I went to swing on the swings. I saw him and I went, timid, me, it was barely dark out, I went, I leaned my bike against the wall of the shack, I approached him, I nodded to him, and I continued toward the swings

Why had I done that?

Trust.

Sheldon Clark, the mysterious boy, was on the bench playing guitar pretty well.

I had learned to play 'Blackbird' with him in September. *Of course, everyone knows how to play 'Blackbird,' but you have a nice voice*, he said after hearing me play guitar with my friends. *I'm taking singing lessons*, I told him. *Lula, Debussy. Singing in French is harder than in Italian*, I told him. He was curious, and I proudly told him that after one year I was starting to sing in French. It was gruelling. I didn't have enough breath, and I didn't think I was a true soprano. I couldn't hit the high notes. I swam to improve my lung capacity, but my jaw was clenched. I had to open up and be the cathedral that receives the sound. *Life is resonant*, I had said. *All of life is in sound.* I didn't know whether he understood. He spoke French well, but he was distracted. I had wondered for a moment whether he was intelligent. You can't always tell right away. I had chased the idea out of my head, stern with myself. I didn't like how I tended to judge the intelligence of others. He was a good guitar player, after all.

Finally he came over.

'They don't take down the swings in the winter,' I said.

It was a ludicrous thing to say, perhaps explaining my presence in the park in spite of the advancing hour.

It wasn't very cold, strangely.

My short brown suede coat, my blue scarf, he left them on.

'Love Street' was easy. I picked it up in a few minutes.

He put his guitar in its case.

I stood to leave, it was getting colder, and then he started to laugh.

'What are you laughing at?'

'Come here,' he said.

He held me by my scarf at first. And then by the hair.

He knocked me down, and I crawled under the swing set.

At first, I saw him pitching. I saw him pitching against the black sky. Then he turned me over to face the ground, and I didn't see anything more.

He broke my arm when I tried to stop him taking off my shoes, and then my jeans.

It was afterwards that he turned me over.

I tried to move my face to protect myself. He lifted my head and smashed it a few times against the rock. I managed to shield myself with my left hand.

It lasted barely a few minutes.

He left, taking his guitar with him.

He hadn't said a word.

It was my voice, my screams that were still reverberating through the park.

Alone, my mind was blank for a moment, I pictured nothing, nothing at all, which meant, maybe, but it wasn't entirely a thought, barely an instinct of death, staying there, that way, for the rest of my life.

And then I thought, *it could have been worse.*

I thought, *I could be dead.*

I got up on my hands and knees and looked for my shoes. My feet were cold, that's what I was thinking. It was November, there was cold dirt in my hair. I wanted to cut it, right then. I wanted to rip my hair out.

I found my shoes under the other swing. I sat down. I put my underwear back on, then my jeans and my shoes, with difficulty because I no longer had the use of my right arm, and my left hand was covered in blood, but after that I didn't have any idea of what to do or where to go. I wasn't far from home, but I didn't know which direction to head in. Should I keep crawling on all fours?

I could picture my mother sitting in the living room in her gold dress. It was 1978, the dresses were pretty, sleeveless, Jackie Kennedy. My mother's hair was blond. She spoke with her pretty Polish accent. I didn't want to hurt her.

I was begging for it not to have happened, not to me, not to her.

I managed to stand up.

'Dad,' I called out.

I knew I was calling into an empty park.

I called out to him anyway.
My father would want to kill him.
'I'll kill him,' he might say.
I called him for that too.
I walked home; it wasn't far.
I don't know why I rang the doorbell.
My father opened the door.

What's your name?
Her name is Ana.
It was my father talking.
My mother, in her nightgown, was crying. My two brothers and sister were awake, somewhere in the house, kept away by one of the police officers.
'We have to get her to the hospital,' my mother said.
She got a grip on herself.
'She needs a doctor,' she insisted.
They called an ambulance. It was better that way, the two police officers said.
She knows him, my father repeated, before sitting down next to me.
He held my hand.
'You know him?'
At that moment, he seemed completely helpless.
My mother was stroking my forehead.
Where's my little sister? I thought.
Where's the cat?
I couldn't talk anymore.
But lying in my hospital bed, after the exam, I had to talk some more.
'What's his name?'
'Was he there when you got there?'
'Did he say anything?'

'Had you arranged to meet him?'
Until they put me to sleep with a strong tranquilizer.

The next morning, when I woke up, I saw the overhead shot of bodies in the jungle.

I saw myself with my coat, my bare legs and no face.

Why wasn't I dead?

Why was I still here?

That's what I was asking myself.

While he, while under the swing set.

Hundreds of people killed like me, no, worse than that, assassinated, hundreds of people already so broken that they preferred to obey. And what were they thinking as they swallowed the poison? Relief? Release? Would I be broken like that for the rest of my life?

My mother and father were at my bedside. They looked at my swollen face. I looked at the TV. It was easier than thinking about myself.

The journalist was talking about finding preparations for a celebration at the site of the massacre.

I had gone to my singing lesson in the afternoon. It was nice out, and I felt like going for a bike ride in the evening. One last time before the snow. I stopped at the park.

I hadn't planned to.

And yet that's the way the world was, suspended, waiting.

And now I was going to have to fight.

I told Inspector Massé what I could. I gave him all the facts. In other words, not much, in the end. But he was sensitive enough to figure out the rest.

Philippe finally went to play outside with the neighbours across the street. The woman had three children and two dogs, and he often went out to join them when he saw them in front of their house. I kept an eye on him while I poured out my past. Philippe, of course, kept an eye on me too, which made the telling of my story a little more relaxed. I had to look detached, for Philippe. I also needed to be able to interrupt myself the second I had to. And I knew that the manner of the telling wouldn't change what had happened: the rest of the story was here, it was me, it was my skin, my bones. It was my head, all the shadows in my head. The memory didn't fade. But I didn't relive it often either. It stayed inside me like a stillborn bird.

The inspector listened to me. He heard the rustling of the bird's wings.

He asked me questions. I answered them. He understood.

The days of hospitalization, the days of waiting, the days of the trial.

'Maybe I didn't fight hard enough,' I said.

If I had grabbed the rock. If I had hit him right in the face.

'But he was convicted. You did the right thing.'

I had indeed won a battle. And an entire life cannot hinge around a single image.

'Of course,' I said. 'Doing the right thing is good. But it's not always enough.'

I got up to be able to see Philippe better. When his eyes met mine, I smiled at him; it was a caress sent above time. We could be that way: two, with the memory of three, but not like a ghost. Simply a good omen.

I went to get some lemonade in the kitchen.

'Philippe made it this morning,' I said.

He took a mouthful of the pink liquid and made a face.

'Too sweet,' he said, putting his glass down on the table.

He was so serious. I wanted to chastise him, but I held back.

'There's one thing that was never made clear,' he said. 'Sheldon Clark, why was he never found?'

That's what he was after. He wasn't all that interested in my pain. Or maybe yes, he was sensitive to it, because perhaps he too was driven by some sort of compulsion. I could relate.

But I was disappointed. It's a feeling I hadn't often felt.

He recognized it.

'Ana, I want to make sure that everything was done by the book back then. What happened when he got out of prison?'

I thought for a moment about how to answer him, what to choose from the chain of events that followed what he had said. What interested him had happened a few days later.

Yes, Sheldon Clark got out of prison.

Happiness was a word I had almost managed to reinvent with Rudi and Philippe. I had a life. Thinking I was protected by this life, I came back to live in this damn neighbourhood to be close to my parents. The houses were cheaper than downtown, and Rudi really liked it. I thought that the past was the past, that he had forgotten about me.

He was waiting for me at the door to the mall.

Even before I saw him, I sensed his presence. The air felt fraught with danger, and then I sensed him. As if the eight years that had just passed had stayed behind the heavy closed door or were stuffed into a corner, under a car, under the shopping buggy of the woman who was crossing the parking lot ahead of me and whom I couldn't ask for help, no matter where, it didn't matter, as long as they left plenty of room for the question: how had I managed to survive?

How had I managed not to die? How had the rest of the world been able to mean anything other than that hour when, unbeknownst to everyone, I had been forced to smother everything I wanted out of life under the weight of a body turned savage?

He moved toward me, smiling.

His body, the body of the man who had raped me, had changed: his arms were now muscular like an athlete's, his face had hardened, he looked more like what was inside him and had exploded that night in November 1978. He pressed me up against the wall.

'You see, I didn't forget you,' he whispered in my ear.

His tongue penetrated further, and I heaved. For a moment I thought I would vomit, and it took everything I had not to.

He didn't intend to hurt me, at least not right away, and he let me go.

He smiled at me again, all excited, as if it were really some sort of reunion.

'I'll be seeing you, eh?'

He waved at me while I caught my breath.

I could see the scene in slow-motion: the director had placed it at the beginning of the film to trick the viewer, and then the scene was shown again when all the pieces of the puzzle were starting to fall into place. I wasn't a character in this story, only a witness. The man's gesture was cheerful, but his eyes were disturbing. The woman was frozen, she was waiting for something but didn't know what. Maybe for the sky to open up above the mall, maybe for everything to be swept away, the rows of parked cars, the people with their bags, the scene itself whirling around in the eye of the cyclone. And then everything would be put back in place, the world would become as it was before, only there would be a little more dust, and after a while we would realize that one person was missing.

I watched him walk away, but I still couldn't quite grasp that this was happening, that this had happened.

A taxi stopped in front of me. No doubt the driver thought I was waiting for him, and I got in.

It was a very short trip, which the driver made sure I knew, and that's when, because of his unkind remarks, I started to shake.

'Okay,' he said.

I mentally recorded every word, as if all of reality were now Sheldon Clark's accomplice, and I would soon be called upon to testify. I had come back down to earth.

I saw the buildings on Boulevard de la Côte-Vertu stream past and I hated the street. I hated myself for having come back here. I had let down my guard.

My mother asked me where my bike was.

I didn't want to talk to her right away, and I told her to go. Rudi was the one who explained to her later what had happened.

Sheldon Clark had been out of prison for a few months. He had probably looked for me, then watched me, maybe for days. He had found my house, he knew where Philippe's kindergarten was, he knew. He had followed me that morning.

I filed a complaint.

The police assured me that they would do everything they could to arrest him and put him back in jail.

But it took too long.

I was too afraid.

'It was so unfair,' I said.

Robert Massé nodded his head in agreement.

'And he was never found?'

'Never.'

'You think he really disappeared?'

'Yes.'

'And you've kept living here, never knowing whether he would come back?'

'What else could I do? We had surveillance at the beginning, and then later, nothing.'

'He never tried to contact you again?'

'Never.'

'So why threaten you then?' he said, his jaw clenched.

'Find him. He can tell you.'

I had nothing more to say.

He made as if to lean in toward me, as if he were waiting for the rest of my confession. Then he changed his mind.

We both knew I was lying, the difference being that I didn't know what truth I was hiding.

'I was protected,' I laughed.

He realized I would go no further. He knew what sort of person I was. He knew that if I were sure of even one thing, I would keep it to myself.

'So everything's all right,' he said.

Philippe came in at that moment and the inspector stood.

'Are you leaving?' Philippe asked.

'I have to get back to work. But thanks for the chess tips.'

Philippe approached him with his hand outstretched.

I love it when he does that. It leaves people at a loss.

I shook the inspector's hand, as if my son had prompted me to.

'Are you sure about Kimi?' Philippe asked.

'Yes, young man.'

Philippe went quiet for a moment, tears in his eyes.

I think he knew full well that we weren't telling him everything, that the everything in question involved me, involved his mother's sadness, a sort of crack never filled in the walls of our house, and I think he had just decided that that's what life would be like: upsetting, implausible, answerless.

'Okay,' he said. 'She must be better off now.'

Robert Massé laid his hand on him. Philippe immediately pulled away, his shoulder bruised.

We went out on the front steps.

'I went to see you to talk about his hairdresser,' I said. 'Not me.'

'It doesn't matter,' he said. 'One thing leads to another, doesn't it?

'Maybe, but not only in the way you think.'

He took my hand again, which he held tight for a moment.

'Take care of the two of you,' he said.

I said goodbye to him one last time, grateful, and I went inside.

I thought of the survivors, about what we were, Philippe, Elliott and me.

'Rudi,' I said.

The day, like the summer, was just beginning. I went to join Philippe in the yard. He gave me a kiss.

'Dad would have liked our flowers,' he said.

'It's true. And Elliott.'

'Not so sure.'

'Come on, Philippe, your father loved animals.'

'He still loves them,' he said.

The sun burst into our yard.

I was happy at that moment.

It was that moment, and not another. And it was everything I could have hoped for.

'What will your life be after me?' Rudi asked.

'And you? What will your life be without me?'

We had come to these last words. They were said with the tenderest of smiles in our voice.

I had wanted to keep Rudi at home until the end, but it was an uphill battle. I didn't have enough time. It all went so fast at the end.

His hospital room was bright, there were wildflowers in vases along the windowsill, drawings by Philippe pinned to the wall. This was it, he was leaving, and I had to go on.

It wasn't the same room, or the same hospital, but I saw myself again in this hell from which I could find no rescue, and I was suddenly so scared of being alone.

'I can't,' I said, resting my head on Rudi's shoulder.

He was dying, and I was still asking him to be there for me.

He stroked my hair weakly.

I stood up and got a hold of myself. Nothing should tarnish the love that was between us, not memory or even death, now raising its great sails.

'I promise you everything will be okay,' he whispered.

'I know,' I said.

Because Rudi always kept his promises.

A few days after I saw Sheldon Clark again, he sat in front of me holding my hands in his, and he swore to me that no one would ever hurt me again. *No one. Ever.* The way he looked at me, his absolute confidence in his powers, everything told me that I should believe him.

'Don't ask questions. Believe in me.'

I could trust him on that; he would never confess anything that would cause me more worry.

I never asked questions.

And so it was that I couldn't completely hide the truth from Inspector Massé. Sheldon Clark had indeed disappeared. But I didn't know under what orders exactly, and I didn't know into what world, and I didn't know how.

But what is truth in the end?

A man had died and a nurse brought a little boy into the room. And the only thing I could understand was the little boy's helplessness as he looked at his father's body.

I was no longer thinking of my pain; I was thinking of nothing, only of holding this little person against me and taking him far away.

And then, our life punctuated by sadness, surprising joy some evenings, our funny little ways, our dreams, our appointment every month with the hairdresser and her silent gestures.

There was a sort of comfort in this routine. I understood the control that Philippe tried to have over his life. The only disruption was our new cat. He brought out emotions we couldn't control. It wasn't his fault that we loved him. It wasn't his fault that he disappeared overnight sometimes. We would go look for him together in the dark. We would call his name in the schoolyard behind the house, both of us aware enough of our peculiar ways. Our hearts had to beat faster sometimes. We had to remember to rail against this fragile life.

'Your dad saved me,' I said.

Love saves, that's want I wanted him to understand. Even if I didn't completely believe it myself.

The inspector had just left, and the sun had enticed Elliott to stretch out at our feet as we lay on a blanket in the middle of the yard.

I turned on my side, my face close to Philippe's.

'Your dad saved me.'

I told him a story, the story of a young girl attacked by a bad man. The young girl is terrified. She feels bad long after what happened, long after the thin scar on her cheek has faded to the point of disappearing, almost, at least to those who don't come too close, but she is surrounded by wonderful people, and one day she finds love. She is still so young. Sometimes, overwhelmed by the sense of danger, she rushes home, praying not to be taken by surprise when the world explodes; she wants to be there, she wants to ward off the advance of the coming catastrophe with her eyes. She is afraid that her little boy feels the same thing. He feels it, she knows, even though he feels it differently, but everything will be all right now, he has to believe. *It's us, okay, it's in us, but nothing else will happen.*

He sat up on the blanket.

'Everything is all right, Philippe, I swear.'

'Then why are you saying it?'

'I have to explain it to you for it to go away.'

'What?'

'The worry.'

'But he came back, Mom.'

'You know about that?'

'Dad told me. It was when I was little, the day you helped the police.'

'You don't forget a thing, do you? Yes, Philippe, he came back. But he was arrested and he won't come back again.'

He looked away, a little angry.

'I imagined things.'

'What things?'

'Things.'

That was us.

'And why did Dad die?'

I thought for the first time that what Rudi didn't tell me may have killed him. I had done as he asked and buried my questions so deep that I had become blind, was that it? Did his promise poison his blood? I don't know, don't know. But I still had the power to calm two minds that were getting carried away.

'It was a disease, Philippe, bad luck. It has nothing to do with the other thing.'

Did I really believe myself? I had to. I had said as much to Inspector Massé, and now I had to defend it: one thing doesn't always lead obviously to another. There is a chain of events, of course. There are things flashing on the web of time. There is a woman who dies, another who survives. There are ghosts who send us silent signals, others who manage to cloak themselves in the night. There are family mythologies within the larger human mythology. But what there isn't is a satisfactory explanation, an absolute, clear-cut answer.

'The world is dangerous,' Philippe said. 'And you're unlucky.'

'Unlucky? Au contraire. I'm lucky. I have you.'

'That's not luck.'

'So what do you call it? I could have ended up with a boring little boy!'

I was trying to cheer him up. It was tough going. But even though his face was turned, I saw the beginnings of a smile.

I would have to tell him more, that much was for sure. But for now, it was enough. I think I had, in a way, just by getting a little closer to him, managed to soothe him.

He got up, went to play with his things, happy to be alone.

That evening we had dinner at my parents'.

Philippe didn't say a word about Inspector Massé's visit. I was surprised. But happy. He seemed to have decided that it belonged to us. He had learned that certain parts of stories were better left between us, in the music of the unfinished, like Kimi's death. We talked about our trip to the Gaspé. My parents were going to join us.

I sketched an itinerary on the cream paper napkin.

'I'll rent a house,' I said.

This time, he believed me.

I can see myself again passing in front of the group of men sitting on the sidewalk by the door of the salon. I can still feel the fear that brushed against my consciousness each time without fully taking form. I drove it away, the fear, still thinking I was misjudging things, an after-effect of the attack that caused my body and mind to clench when faced with a potential rapist.

What it was was a premonition.

I can see Kimi's beautiful face again.

'Guyana,' she said.

But I wasn't listening.

If I had listened to her, if I had even listened to my own fatigue, it would have made me pay way more attention to Kimi's words. If I had truly looked into her eyes and tried to pierce the silence that always accompanied her smile, maybe she wouldn't have died.

'Guyana,' she would have said.

Her eyes would have sparkled with fabrication and I would have recognized it.

It wasn't an island. It wasn't paradise either.

My own memories would have immediately taken on the dull taste and smell of the massacre in the jungle, a few hours before the rotting began.

'Yes, but your country isn't really paradise,' I would have said.

Would she have kept smiling and telling me about the sun, the fruit trees and the sweet smell of soy milk?

I think so, at first.

She would have gathered Philippe's hair firmly but tenderly behind his head. She would have held the comb so that it gathered a clump of hair while gently scraping the scalp. Like you would do with a cat. And then there would have been the gap, the secret second between her and the world.

'You have such a handsome boy,' she would have said quickly.

She wanted so badly to bring me back to life, to my present life, right away.

I would have insisted, forced my way into the corridors of that secret second.

'Wasn't Jonestown in Guyana?'

Maybe this time she would have let some of her reserve fall.

She would have lost some of it, I'm sure. A burning wind would have carried it away, just like it carried the dark rumour between the trunks of the palm trees.

'That was in the jungle, Ana,' she would have said.

Then she would have shared a bit of what she was with me. Her dead brother, her shame for her cousin's murderers. And the memory of the massacre that threw everything into disarray.

'We all went a little crazy after that,' she would have said, shaking her head.

Our pasts would have met somewhere in the image of a thousand people lying face down in the dirt in the jungle. We were made of these deaths too.

Maybe if I hadn't waited so long before telling her, before confiding in her what had happened to me that was worse than Rudi's death, the violence that I knew I would partially unwrap in front of her, later on, not right away, the violence I was never ready to talk about, even though I knew that if I were to ever again, it would be with her, extracting a piece of the horror from a black mass. I would bring up the incident like a piece of far-off news, hoping, however, that she would understand, that she would wrap me in understanding silence, the impossible, what even Rudi could not do, wrapped up in his anger, in his will to find an explanation, a solution, a shelter for his own demons. I knew she was capable of that, in any case, and maybe if I had spoken earlier, she wouldn't be dead.

First I would have let her cut my hair.

If I had left myself in her hands, my reserve would have dried up like the skin of a snake in the sun.

She would have confided her doubts about Wilson, and I would have told her what I thought.

She would have left before it was too late, not to have to hear from her fiancé's mouth what was going down in the salon or, just in time, she would have asked me for help. Because she would have known what I had been through.

I would have been there for her.

There wouldn't have been that overwhelming, sudden solitude before which she would submit at the end.

Would that have changed anything?

I still like to think so.

The Smile of Silence

Yes, the little boy came in with his mother one day in June. He wanted to have his hair cut for his father's funeral. Handsome as anything. A real movie star.

Since I've been gone, I see him as a little brother. His mother, Ana, is always in the background, a shadowy silhouette in the bedroom of a child who's a little bit scared. And my brother, whom I will be joining soon.

I'm looking forward to that day, because there is too much solitude here; I'm trapped between two worlds.

But it's for Ana that I'm remembering this moment.

Hairdressers know everything, I told her little boy.

Women hairdressers even more, I should have added. Right then, I already knew enough to fear the worst. But the two of them were a breath of fresh air in the salon.

His mother went out, and the boy was as stiff as a board in the chair, his eyes watery like a puppy's.

I could feel that a torrent of tears was about to explode from him, like a cloud heavy with rain. I know a thing a two about torrential rain. The flooded streets, the mud running down the mountains, your body pricked by little warm needles, welcome for a moment and then resented the rest of the day. I had to be careful.

Hairdressers can read minds, I said. You feel like crying?

The little boy and his big eyes didn't answer but found the dam to stop his tears.

He laughed, to show that he didn't believe me.

It's just something we do, I said. Sometimes we pretend we're psychologists.

I hate psychologists, he said.

Is that so?

I was combing his hair and gathering it behind his head.

Me too, I said.

He told me how the school psychologist had stroked his hair and how he didn't trust anyone who did that.

Imagine what it'll be like at my dad's funeral, he said.

So we'll cut it really short, I said.

That was the most important moment: offering the little boy a bit of solace.

He looked like a pale Tom Cruise.

His mother came back in, looked at her marvellous little boy and burst out laughing.

Well, you're even more handsome than before, she said, admiring her son in the mirror.

She didn't dare touch him.

It was odd.

They were alike: their gestures started and then stalled in mid-air, as if refusing to go any further, as if going further would mean throwing them both to the ground.

I recognized this sort of distance. With my brother dead, all of my parents' gestures had retreated and stayed caught in an impasse.

This recognition took root in them, and they came back to see me every month. The boy couldn't stand it when his hair wasn't just so. In that he was the opposite of his mother.

The second time they came in, she told me about Philippe's father, her husband.

I didn't tell her I already knew.

The little boy smiled at me, in on the secret.

And then he told his mother that she could leave. The habit was already established in his mind. But she told him she preferred to stay. He was disappointed, but he didn't show it.

Ana watched me work. It gave her a chance to focus her world on this little scene where gestures are precise.

I love the sound of scissors, she told me one day.

Snip snip snip.

Particularly on boys' hair.

I knew what she meant. Scissors move faster over short hair. It feels like hundreds of little strokes of ice skates. Shick shick shick. Cold, clear, precise. You know where to go, and you go there. Then when you take off the cape, suddenly there is new light on the face. This is why I wanted so badly to cut Ana's hair. I wanted her face to light up like a straw-coloured moon appearing from behind a cloud. Her sadness was tucked behind a curtain. She was protecting her son. She was protecting herself. I don't think it was very good for either of them. Me, I held my head so high that my past in Guyana suffocated under the dead hair around my chair. I swept it up; I swept the dirt on the miniature veranda, I swept the dust on the kitchen floor, I swept up my mother's fears and my father's helplessness. I forgot my little sisters, slaves to the one event that had managed to contain all the others. My brother killed by a policeman and the rest of our lives exploding into a thousand particles of stories of murder. I forgot the domination, I swept up Wilson's blindness, I did my work in the hair salon with no customers. I thought about going back to Guyana.

I went back.

But not as I'd hoped.

Anyhow, nobody leaves Guyana or goes back there completely alive. Or completely dead, it seems.

When I was born, everyone was still talking about the three Mirabal sisters assassinated in the Dominican Republic on November 25, 1960.

The murders sparked hate speech that infiltrated the cracks in the sidewalks like rainwater, that stagnated in the mud around the markets and homes. I was born in 1967, but the story lived in the shadow of my past. My mother talked about it with my aunts. It was background music. She traced the story back to the twenty-three women killed by their husbands in the 1860s – the ghosts of these women still roamed the pile dwellings. What sort of slavery was this? There was also the fire that had ravaged our neighbour's house during the riots. Fear was ingrained in me, as if I had to get down on my knees before the adversary could strike. It was as if the seawall had held back the present, as if the past came and went along the canals. So, even before my birth, I was one in a line of neglected, mistreated women. Our world had changed, of course. But some roots are hard to rip up. When my cousin Sattie was found dead on the seawall, my mother, who was standing in the kitchen, started screaming and didn't stop the entire evening. Sattie had been raped and killed, beaten with a club. Her face was all blue, it seems, her little yellow dress torn and covered in blood. My mother put her hands over my ears and then she started screaming. When she let me go, my cheeks were red and creased, and she kept screaming. Then my father arrived and held her in his arms for a long time. He made her tea and made me a bowl of sweet rice. Aria and Lydie came home from school with my older brother, Daniel. I had stayed home because I had a stomach ache, which is why I saw everything. My mother calmed down. She went to spend the evening at her sister's house, the mother of Sattie, my dead cousin just a little older than me. And that's when everything started to burn in our house, as if the others had set fire to it.

My father, gentle soul that he was, did not try to find the guilty parties. Anyway, we knew. The police had made their rounds, as had the rumours.

My mother was angry. Resignation came later, as with my brother's death.

For my death, too, it will come.

My mother will iron her pretty fabrics more slowly than normal while smoothing her thoughts. My father will watch her from a distance, no longer daring to approach her. One night, they will go out onto the veranda. They will sit side by side in the old love seat. The smell of rice will waft through the window as usual, but it will be different, with a hint of the unfamiliar. My father will take my mother's hand, and she will finally give in. I will manage to brush against them with my cool breath, one second, a single tiny second; they will both think about this damn country that drains its dark waters into our dreams, they will think of me and smile again with their sad smiles.

November was so painful.

So ominous.

It was the beginning of the rainy season. Everyone was waiting for the floods with a gleam of defiance in their eyes. I wasn't worrying too much about the future. Our house could withstand anything, why think otherwise? It was solid, even on a strip of land below sea level. I thought that my whole life would unfold here. I was still a little girl, very small for my age. And very sensible. Except when I was hanging around with my friends at the Stabroek Market, which drove my mother to distraction.

After Sattie's murder, there were a number of other rapes. All the victims were Indians, Metis, coolies. A journalist wrote a series of articles about the rapes, at the same time denouncing the reign of terror instituted by the government, and he was killed. That's when the riots that took my brother broke out. The look in his eye had changed since Sattie's death. He had always had the same loving eyes as our father, but now he no longer looked at me. I didn't know where my brother Légende was anymore. Then he was shot by Burnham's police, who used their weapons at will. Play-acting at justice afterward, of course. No charges were laid. My brother the hero, his soul prisoner of the Guyana sky. Now I'm here to free him. Him, and my parents, and my two little sisters grieving for me in their new lives.

The riots and my brother's death soon dropped out of the headlines in Guyana. Another event dominated the news, and the images of chaos on television and in the newspapers forever coloured my view of humanity. There had been rumours circulating for some time about what was going on at Port Kaituma, but I found that out only afterwards. At the time I was too young to make out the sound of the horror that was looming. There were still horrible, thundering tragedies reverberating right beside me. But they were still something you could grasp, orderly, if you will, if the word means anything; Sattie's death, my brother's anger and death, two events that separate and come together again in the same nest of sorrow like two branches of a river.

Everyone knew that Jonestown had been built a few years earlier, but we still called it Port Kaituma. Of course, nobody visited anyone in Jonestown. Except probably friends of the government and maybe even Forbes Burnham himself. No one knew what was going on there. A sort of revolutionary village in the jungle bearing the name of its leader and creator. Cousins of cousins sometimes saw Jim Jones at the Pegasus Hotel, at his headquarters, on the streets of Georgetown, in the company of government officials. The rumours came and went. Until November 18, 1978.

Bodies, and bodies, and more bodies, seen from above by helicopters.

At first, no one knew what they had died of. Some sort of epidemic? The police had chased fugitives into the jungle. Fugitives from what? In the jungle? Dissident members assassinated, Leo Ryan assassinated at the Port Kaituma airport – this was happening right around me – there were policemen, cousins of cousins, who went to deal with the bodies rotting in the sun, maybe no sun, maybe not quite rain yet, but an odour of the end of the world in a paradise ruled by the deranged.

Everyone was talking about the massacre then, but where was my brother? What did he think? Could he still see me? Could he see his little sister suddenly doubting even the living presence of her parents?

Standing in front of the television, in the middle of the living room. Disbelieving, like them, my mother and father ordering me half-heartedly out of the room, as immobile as two Caribbean flamingos balanced in muddy water. My two little sisters also trying to get me to go outside. But I didn't want to go outside anymore. There was a tide of human beings in the jungle not far from us, still warm in the hot dust. Their tormented souls could float to my house and touch me, like all the terrible stories that had touched me since my birth. These souls hadn't learned to die yet. There was my brother, half gone too, who wanted to defend the honour of Sattie and the future of his little sisters. I heard him yelling that to my father, that it couldn't happen again, that this shouldn't happen to his sisters.

I believed that these events were now connected. The precarious order of my little life, thrown into disarray by images on TV. If you could die that way, if Forbes Burnham could allow that to happen, if our gods could order it. Sattie, my brother and then almost a thousand people. Was this what war was?

We saw the photos everywhere, we turned on the television and saw the face of Jim Jones, his black hair shining even under cloud cover, we heard his speeches: Become good revolutionaries, he kept saying over and over. We saw the bodies that had been rotting for three days. I didn't understand any of it. I saw a pile of bodies, that was all. They were twisted like rope, as if they were intertwined, the children too, with little shoes at the end of their little legs – most of them, we would learn later, would never be identified. What war had this been?

And then, after a few weeks, a few days even, it all levelled off, as if a steamroller had flattened the entire country.

My parents were able to get back to their grief. But each on their own side of an invisible boundary that now divided the house in two. My mother's anger. The shame of my father, who felt a bit of cowardice for accepting things as they were.

The ghosts of the children awaiting their revenge. And I had started grieving for something else; I knew that one day I would have to leave this place. I kept the secret like a delicate tree planted in my head for years.

My sisters left first to go work in the United States, and they both married, to the great relief of my parents. Almost at their request, I should say. I stayed behind to help in the store. I didn't mind. I liked being surrounded by colourful fabric. I liked spreading cheer. I stored up warmth in a still-invisible place in my body. I pretended nothing crazy had happened, not in the house, not in the world.

My secret bore fruit, which I one day offered to my parents, when I was certain that they could stay on their own, the anger and the shame having slowly ebbed, the ghost of Daniel now resting in a truly legendary country, in the shadow of the house, in the shadow of my new life.

I arrived in Montreal in the cold, and my memories froze, just like I wanted them to, instantly, like little animals captured and kept in a freezer, frosted silhouettes.

When Wilson asked me to marry him, I didn't say yes right away. He didn't really even ask me to marry him. He kept me warm all winter with his big Jamaican body perfectly integrated with this grey city; in the spring he gave me the ring, pretending it was a diamond. I pretended to believe him. I said yes. Yes to nothing. Yes to him warming my body. Yes to the ways of a boy who thinks he is as hard as steel and has conquered the world, who believes he is on the side of the conquerors.

It's not an engagement, he explained when he saw my surprise.

His arms sliced through the air as if chasing away an evil spirit.

He thought for a moment.

But maybe it is, he added.

The kiss that followed sealed the lie.

That was how Wilson was. He let ambiguity take over and create a second version of reality. This is why I didn't see him for what he was. I never even managed to see myself for what I was. Not telling each other the truth was a passion of ours. Until the moment I walked in on him exchanging bags of drugs for money. Until the moment when the other boys saw what I had seen. They were in a circle with Wilson at the centre, like a commander preparing his soldiers for combat. Or, rather, like a gamemaster, because it was a game – the boys were weak, even Wilson was weak in this gangster-movie masquerade.

But they saw me, and they all stopped talking, and one of them glared at me.

So Wilson's not the gang leader, I said to myself.

And I stayed there, waiting for my fiancé to react.

Barely a few seconds passed before I understood that he would do nothing, that I had to look away, lower my eyes, show my weakness.

Don't tell me the salon is your cover, I told Wilson later when we were alone.

Don't tell me this is serious, I said.

Don't tell me that.

My hands were trembling.

He was shaking his head more than usual.

You're a child, an idiot, I said.

I still thought it could be fixed. I didn't get that other people were connected to this. That even Wilson and his friends didn't know where they were in the chain of command. That they could lose control of what they were doing and carry me along with them.

I was alone, in my bedroom, with him.

He was one of them, one of those people who could lose control, become someone else.

Besides, he wasn't saying anything terribly smart.

I no longer knew whether he was smart.

And he wasn't that strong after all.

I remember the little boy's mother, Ana, looking at him, the first time she saw him.

Of course, she was older than me, and he looked a bit like a teenager.

But Ana, at least her eyes, your eyes, Ana, didn't judge people that way. It wasn't the judgment, it was the distance. No, not the distance, it was the premonition. It's all clearer now.

And how am I supposed to keep working at the salon? I asked Wilson.

He didn't know it yet, but I couldn't.

What difference does it make to you? he said.

What difference does it make? Now I know. I can't pretend I don't and be an accomplice.

I couldn't do that. I knew it almost right away, although it was completely unexpected.

Wilson ended up promising me that he would find a way to fix it. Maybe at the time he thought that he loved me enough.

It was the last time I saw him.

They came into the salon the next evening after my last appointment.

Two friends of Wilson's whose names I didn't know. He had never introduced them. I had never asked him why. I didn't want my conscious mind to know what I knew. I was lying to myself. Wilson was lying. I was guilty of being blind as well.

They said hello and told me to finish up my work.

I swept. I emptied the little wastebasket of grey hair into a bag. I put everything away.

I was trembling like a weakling, someone refusing to recognize her own strength. Because I'm strong, and I've always known it. I know. My brother murdered, my parents, my escape, my little sisters abandoned. My own violence held in check like evidence of a murder in the false bottom of a suitcase.

The cash, one of them said.

I thought they wanted the money, and for a moment I was relieved. I held out what there was. A thin wad of bills.

A salon for the poor, I thought for the first time. Of course, poverty in this country is relative. The sick old lady's grey hair looked up at me. The whole salon took on a grey tinge, a dirty grey, with no highlights. It was my life, the one I had chosen.

They started laughing.

Did I really think they had come for the money?

Such a paltry sum when their pockets were already full?

One of them threw a hundred-dollar bill in my face.

That was when I asked myself why Wilson wasn't there. He had always come to wait for me at the salon door.

I understood in the same sharp turn of my thoughts that he wasn't the one I would call if I needed help. Not him, not Harriet. No one. I was the loneliest fiancée in the world.

You want more?

Like an imbecile, he made the change in his pocket jingle.

I tried to talk to them.

I started to defend myself, to defend Wilson.

It seemed to confuse them.

They had come to threaten me and I was lecturing them?

Wasn't I scared?

I'm scared, I said.

Are you sure you're scared enough?

Yes, I'm scared. I'll never say anything to anyone.

What's Wilson doing with this stupid bitch?

They laughed again.

I could tell from their laughter that they were high.

They were flying, as a matter of fact.

They inhabited a different space and time than me. They were balanced precariously on a wire in a bubble. Excited, like they were engaged in an extreme sport.

They're dangerous, I thought then.

You wouldn't have thought so to look at them. They looked like big teenagers showing off, like Wilson.

But they were dangerous because of their own fear.

So, you going to turn us in to the police? one of them said.

I shook my head.

Go ahead, pick up the phone and call.

Only one of them was doing the talking.

The other one pulled out a knife and pointed it at me.

I started to cry.

Not a lot, just enough to irritate them.

The rest happened in a sort of fog.

Time moved slowly. I didn't know what they wanted. The one doing the talking paced back and forth. The other one sat in my chair, still holding the knife.

They turned on the radio. That got them even more excited. They looked like they were going to start dancing.

For a moment I thought they would leave. They really seemed to be having a good time, and I told myself they would finish the evening somewhere else.

But they stayed.

This was where they wanted to be, with the girl who was me, without Wilson.

Their eyes now told me.

Me, crushed by fear. Preferring to die than to go through what I thought they were going to do to me.

I was casting panicked glances outside, telling myself that someone would walk by soon. This sort of naive hope always crops up at the end, and it was doing its work. It was radiant, not fleeting – it was almost soothing me.

The café next door probably wasn't closed; someone would leave and see what was going on and come help me.

Who was going to save me?

When the phone rang, I thought of little Philippe who hadn't been in in a while. School would be almost over, and I thought it was his mother calling for his beginning-of-summer appointment. I don't know why I thought of them rather than someone else. I should have seen my family flash before my eyes, my mother, my father; I should have pleaded to my sisters, prayed to my dead brother. Instead, I saw the little boy and his mother coming in through the door with the sunlight, even though it was dark. Maybe thoughts connect in some way; they think about me, I know it now, like I know they were close to saving my life. They could have if they had arrived earlier. They could have come, invited me to the school party, I could have decided not to say anything to Wilson. They needed me, in any case. They were both pretty big on ritual: you don't finish a year with scruffy hair, you don't celebrate your birthday without a new dress, etc. It made sense that they would call at that moment. They needed me, and I couldn't do anything more for them. I had practically abandoned them. I thought of the only time I cut Ana's hair. It didn't help. I thought of her vulnerability when she told me what she had been through. I thought of young girls subjugated, I saw my cousin and I saw myself, because now I was in the clutches of men who were defending a territory that simply didn't exist.

Just the ends, she had said.

I burst out laughing, although I was a little disappointed.

I wanted to make her even more beautiful than she was or, rather, I wanted to let her beauty shine through. I always thought that she wanted to tone it down in a way. She turned off the light of her face, and that way her past withdrew into the shadows as well. And that was just it, that was what she wanted, to turn off some of her power, and that day I knew why.

Flipping through a newspaper and suddenly stopping at a headline: *I was raped too.*

Laying the newspaper gently on the counter,

I'm sorry I said that, Kimi. I never say that.

I was seventeen, she added.

My cousin Sattie, I muttered. *Fourteen.*

My heart was beating fast.

It wasn't a confidence. I didn't know what it was, maybe just sharing a reality that inevitably connected, in the past or the future, the existence of every woman on the planet. She looked as surprised as I did, in any case. I saw Sattie pass in front of the mirror for a moment, my vivacious cousin, her brand-new pristine yellow dress that set off her brown skin so nicely. I saw the yellow dress float by on its own, like a ceremonial garment in a museum. I closed my eyes. And then I brushed Ana's hair, the mother of the little boy, I brushed it like I brushed my own when it was long, evenings when the world was too hard, a caress you give yourself, to a part of your body that is easy to heal.

It was a long time ago, she said.

So I had cut her hair, very carefully, but a little shorter than she asked. It was prettier.

Sometimes you have to decide for the customer, I told her.

She looked at herself in the mirror, shaking her head.

But I could tell she was pleased.

Hairdressers always do that, Kimi, she said. *They do as they please.*

She was laughing now. Was she relieved to have confided in me?
Probably not. I had given her a reason to smile though.

I felt so close to her in that moment. Closer than I have ever felt to
anyone. And now I know it was mutual.

Next time, you can do whatever you want, she said.
Outside, on the sidewalk, she hugged me for the first time.
I'll come back soon with Philippe.
But of course, she couldn't come back.
And it was because of Wilson.

The man who wasn't talking found a rope in the backroom.

He made a noose, positioned the little stool and stood on it to hang
the rope.

The other one understood.

He took the knife and ordered me to get up on the stool and put the
rope around my neck.

It was just to scare me some more.

They didn't think I would die, I knew it, but there you have it —
suddenly, or maybe it had been inside me for a long time, regardless, I
was no longer terribly attached to life.

I say that today, but in the moment, it wasn't that. I didn't have time
to think.

It was a reflex of anger, a gesture of revolt.

I saw them laughing.

They laughed.

Until I kicked the stool away with my feet, hard.

I suffocated quickly, and the sound it made forever changed what
they thought they were.

My body returned to the secrets of my death, which are secret only for the
living.

I'm not interested in truth. Facts exist, I leave them be, and they
speak for themselves.

If I'm seeing it all, if I'm recalling the facts, it's for Ana.

I know that she is connected to me with an invisible chain.

I know she heard the silence of my smile.

I see her holding out her hand.

I can't take it, nor can I tell her I'm not dead yet.

But I can look back at everything.

I can look back at everything so intently that she'll know what to do.

Her little boy is with her; they made the transition to summer.

On the table, the dregs of a meal have caught the cat's eye. He approaches, then stops, watchful, having heard Philippe running on the stairs.

He dreamed of his mother in the morning.

Now you're in my dreams, he told her, little architect of reality.

Then he wrapped his arms around her, crying.

I want Dad, he told her again.

Me too, said Ana, careful not to go too far, not to have this moment of grace tumble into a well of questions.

The day goes on, the days will go on, and she won't learn any more about his dream.

The two of them think I hold all the secrets, but it's not true.

I want to tell them that.

To soothe them a little.

I don't have any secrets. Not like Ana's, at any rate.

I want to look back at her past and fuse it with mine.

I adore them and I want my adoration to make their lives clearer.

Was I alive?

Oh yes, I was, extraordinarily alive.

I still am.

But there are still things that taunt me.

I don't know, for example, who grabbed me first. This detail eludes me like you would dismiss the oppressive existence of a crime that wasn't actually committed. But it taunts me like hands starting to strangle me all over again in the dark. Soon, thankfully, the hands will disappear completely and I'll be able to join my brother.

There were two of them, and I hanged myself with their rope as if they had given me the gift of death. My shoes dropped to the floor, which saddened me, and I suffocated. I heard the name Wilson in my head. That's what I would have said, maybe, if I could draw a little air into my lungs. It wasn't him.

But Wilson was silent. He was silent, and I will send no sign to earth to console him.